DEC   2004

F
Hanson, Vic J.
Trail wolves

TRAIL WOLVES

It was a black day for the small town of Lagos. First the bank had been robbed and a teller killed, then a stranger, Tom Brenner, rode in with the corpse of the much-loved Charlie Bennett on his horse. A posse was formed, but no trace of the robbers was found and suspicion fell on Brenner. There were just too many things about this mysterious stranger that didn't add up. If Tom was to clear his name and help catch the killers, he would need all his skills — for death was around every corner.

VIC J. HANSON

TRAIL WOLVES

Complete and Unabridged

LINFORD
Leicester

First hardcover edition published in
Great Britain in 2003 by
Robert Hale Limited, London

Originally published in paperback as
Trail Wolves by Vern Hanson

First Linford Edition
published 2004
by arrangement with
Robert Hale Limited, London

British Library CIP Data

Hanson, Vic J.
   Trail wolves.—Large print ed.—
   Linford western library
   1. Western stories
   2. Large type books
   I. Title II. Hanson Vern
   823.9'14 [F]

   ISBN 1–84395–457–5

Published by
F. A. Thorpe (Publishing)
Anstey, Leicestershire

Set by Words & Graphics Ltd.
Anstey, Leicestershire
Printed and bound in Great Britain by
T. J. International Ltd., Padstow, Cornwall

This book is printed on acid-free paper

1

'I've got a body outside on my horse,' said the stranger. 'Mebbe somebody can identify it an' tell me what to do with it.'

The voice was flat in the stillness.

There had been silence before he entered the saloon. The silence was still there but there was a different feel about it now.

Coney, the owner, pressed his big soft belly into the rim of the bar and his piggy eyes swelled as much as they were able. For once he was at a loss for words. He tried to keep one eye on the stranger while the other revolved to take in the other three men in the saloon.

The two nondescript loafers at the table were of little help. They just gaped. Only Lemmy Dricourt, the middle-aged blacksmith, sagging hugely

1

on the other side of the bar a few yards away, seemed unmoved. Lemmy was, as usual, slightly drunk, and, to the inebriated, things are either solemn or wildly hilarious. Seemed like Lemmy hadn't quite made up his mind about this particular situation — but he wasn't going to let the fact worry him.

He turned and, like a man toeing the white line, crossed the floor towards the door. The two loafers exchanged glances then scrambled in his wake. The stranger followed, and Coney, taking time to squeeze out from behind the bar, brought up the rear.

He noticed the stranger had a nasty limp in his right leg. The stranger had been young, but not too young and with oldish eyes peering sardonically from a sweat-grimed face. He was lean and he walked young and his gimpy leg didn't seem to make much difference to the big gun that jolted in its holster against his right thigh.

'Mebbe you ought to've had a drink first,' Coney wheezed.

Without pausing in his hippitty stride, the stranger half-turned his head.

'It'll keep,' he said. Then, with Coney at his heels, he passed out on to the boardwalk.

The two men halted there, blinking in the brassy sunlight after the gloom of the saloon, looking down at the other three gathered around the horse at the tie-rail. Across the saddle a shapeless bundle was slung. Spare wiry strands of white hair, glinting here and there in the sunlight, brushed a dusty stirrup. Lemmy Dricourt grasped a hank of hair and lifted the head. He grunted explosively as he bent his huge bulk and looked at the face. What he saw seemed to sober him considerably. His movements were more gentle as he lowered the head.

He straightened up. There was no extravagant grunt from him this time. 'It's Charlie Bennett,' he said softly. 'Old Charlie Bennett.'

The stranger went past him then and

unhitched the rope which held the body to the saddle. Then he lifted the body down, cradling it in his arms. He climbed on to the boardwalk and Coney stood aside. The stranger's limp was more pronounced now, as he led the way. At Coney's gesture he laid the body on a bench beneath the window. Lemmy Dricourt folded a small Indian mat and put it beneath the grey head, the lined and peaceful face which belied the ruddy violence of the huge drying stain on the faded shirt-front. Maybe Charlie had seen the one who killed him. Maybe Charlie had died slowly, giving him his chance to forgive. He had been the forgiving sort. Maybe he had figured that, in his philosophy, there was nothing else to do. He had about four slugs in him the stranger said. Enough to kill anyone, even a hard-bitten desert rat like Charlie.

Up till now Lemmy and the stranger had done all the talking. Lemmy deeply and sadly, for Charlie had been his

4

friend; the stranger, tonelessly, noncommittally. Now Coney gave the latter a sidelong glance from his piggy eyes and said:

'The sheriff's outa town. I guess I better do the honours, huh?'

Neither man answered him. Lemmy crossed to the bar and poured himself a drink from the bottle he had left there. The gesture was mechanical. It didn't mean anything anymore. He slid the bottle along the bar and the stranger took it and a clean glass from the rim.

The two men drank. Coney went back behind the bar and faced them. The stranger emptied his glass. 'My name's Brenner — Tom Brenner,' he said.

The two other men introduced themselves. Nobody offered to shake hands. Lemmy turned his head. 'Them two skunks have high-tailed to spread the news,' he growled.

'Tell me about this Charlie Bennett,' said Brenner.

There was little to tell. Lemmy told

it, while Coney stood and glowered. He figured he ought to be the one asking the questions.

When Lemmy had finished Brenner spoke again. 'I figured he was a prospector all right. I was near the hills. I was rounding a bluff when I heard the shots, a whole barrage of 'em. But when I got out into the open again I couldn't see anythin'. The sun was comin' up an', what with the haze an' the dust, visibility wasn't too good. I almost rode over the old man's body. He died as I reached him. He didn't have a chance to say a word. I didn't see anything — not even his horse or burro an' if there was any saddle-bags they'd gone too. The old man didn't have a thing in his pockets an' not even a gun or rifle.'

'You think maybe he was robbed, huh?' said Coney.

Tom Brenner looked directly at the fat man. 'What would you've thought, friend?' he asked softly.

Coney's lips went suddenly dry. The stranger's eyes, a dark greenish grey if they were any colour at all, seemed to burn like a slow fuse. The slightest thing might fan the fuse to a swiftly licking flame: the man looked like he'd explode at the slightest provocation.

Coney said: 'I guess maybe Charlie made a lucky strike an' somebody got to know about it. Or maybe it was just a saddle-tramp riding through who figured he'd come across some easy pickings . . . '

The fat man dried up suddenly, aware once more of the scrutiny of those eyes. Maybe he had said a little too much. After all, wasn't Tom Brenner, or whatever he called himself, just a saddle-tramp passing through? Unless he was aiming to call on somebody here in Lagos.

Lemmy Dricourt scraped a foot in the sawdust and spoke up suddenly. 'I never knew Charlie to make a goodish strike before. Just trickles. Enough to keep him in fodder, an' a coupla nights in town here every now an' then.'

'There's allus a first time for

everything,' said Coney with a sideways glance at Tom Brenner, as if his remark compensated for any innuendo which may have been contained in his previous words.

He jerked his head up as the batwings swung open. The two nondescript loafers reappeared and the foremost one said, 'Jay Simmonds is on his way here.'

'I thought he was outa town,' said Coney.

The second loafer said, 'He came back for provisions. Him an' the sheriff got up into the buttes then lost the trail. The sheriff's still holed up there tryin' to pick up sign.'

Lemmy Dricourt guffawed loudly but without mirth. Then, as all eyes were swivelled in his direction, dropped his head, fondled his drink once more.

More people were trickling into the saloon, glancing a little apprehensively at the group against the bar then swelling the ranks before the body of Charlie Bennett.

All eyes turned towards Jay Simmonds as he entered, his vest thrown open to prominently reveal the deputy's star on his breast. He was big, dark, florid. Florid in every way. He had brushed his clothes well since returning from the hills and the silver ponchoes which fringed his chaps shone brassily and jingled when he walked. It was whispered that Jay was half-Mexican — though the last man who had spoken the thought too loudly and in the deputy's hearing too, had been pistol-whipped to within an inch of his life.

Simmonds' eyes were bold and a little choleric as he surveyed the group by the bar before turning towards the larger bunch around the bench beneath the window. If he noticed the stranger he made no sign of the fact. The second group broke before him and he bent to examine the body of the old prospector.

Not much of this was needed. Simmonds' movements were studiously deliberate as he straightened up, turned. 'Who found him?' he said.

It was an unnecessary question. He had obviously already taken heed of the stranger of whom he had been told. His voice was resonant: it brought the desired effect. Nobody answered the question: everybody looked towards the stranger, who finished rolling himself a smoke and lighting it before he said, 'I'm the one who found the body, Sheriff.'

Simmonds' eyes narrowed suspiciously. 'I'm not the sheriff,' he said. 'I'm in charge while he's away.'

'Same thing,' said Tom Brenner, his head wreathed in blue smoke.

Simmonds moved closer, his head thrust forward a little as if he was striving to peer more closely through that nebulous blue veil.

'Ain't I seen you somewhere before?' he asked.

2

His voice was unfriendly, tinged with the arrogance of his authority. Folks said that he would like to be sheriff. But the regular badge-toter was a tenacious old buzzard, reliable, not so ready to use his gun as was his younger assistant. Between them they balanced things pretty evenly, the older man's caution tempering the younger's pugnacious arrogance.

When his superior was not around, Jay Simmonds was inclined to be overbearing. Now he had a murder-case all to himself and a mysterious stranger, to boot.

Or was he a stranger?

'The name's Tom Brenner. I get around a lot but can't remember ever having seen you before.'

'Where you from?'

'Like I said — I'm a fiddle-foot.'

The voices were toneless now: the men might have been reading dialogue from a play script. They were poor actors.

Or maybe they were good actors. Or, at least, good poker-players.

Simmonds moved to the bar a few yards away from Brenner and stood with one foot on the rail. He placed his left hand on the bar and snapped his fingers, a sign to Coney that he desired his usual drink. His other hand dangled very close to the low-slung gun at his hip.

Coney gave him his drink. He raised his glass. 'I'm glad to meet you, Mr Brenner.'

'Likewise,' said Brenner.

He too lifted the brimming glass that Coney seemed to have inserted beneath his fingers. Coney had two slow fuses on his hands now and he didn't want a wholesale explosion.

'Maybe you'd like to tell me how all this happened, Mr Brenner,' said Simmonds.

Brenner told his story again, in the same unemotional manner. When he had finished, the deputy was taking his second drink. He placed his empty glass carefully on the bar with his left hand and said:

'You better come down to the office with me, Mr Brenner.'

'What for?'

'I'd like to go into this matter further with you.'

'I ain't goin' anywhere yet. I'll stick around.'

'I'm afraid I've got to ask you to accompany me, Mr Brenner.'

Simmonds' voice was still toneless, he might have been a croupier tolling the odds. But now his fingers actually brushed the handle of his gun as he still peered suspiciously at Brenner as if trying to place him in his mind.

Brenner swivelled a little and rested his elbows on the bar. His gun-hand was free now, the gun within easy reach, although he would have had to turn further in order to actually face

Simmonds. If he was aware of this fact, if he realized his danger it did not seem to worry him much. He leaned negligently on the bar and turned his head a little more so that he could see Simmonds.

People were instinctively moving back, leaving a clear space for the two men. All that could be heard now was the stealthy scraping of feet, but neither Brenner or the deputy seemed to notice this.

Simmonds said, 'Have a drink with me before we go will you, Mr Brenner?'

'I'll have a drink,' said Brenner. 'Thanks.'

It was obvious to everybody present that Simmonds' gesture hadn't been a friendly one. The jeering undertone in his voice had been unmistakable, though Brenner didn't seem to have noticed it. He took up his refilled glass from the bar and raised it towards Simmonds in silent toast. The deputy lifted his own glass and moved forward until he stood at the stranger's side. He raised his glass to his lips then, with a flick of his wrist, tossed its contents into Brenner's face.

His other hand moved downwards swiftly, reaching, not for his own gun, but for the other man's. He missed his mark: the gun wasn't there any more. It was in Brenner's hand and, as the lean young man stepped back with liquor streaming down his face, the muzzle of the gun levelled at Simmonds' belly.

Brenner seemed to be consumed by some inward fury which made his body quiver even while his gunhand remained perfectly steady.

'Drop the glass,' he said huskily. 'Make it fast.'

The glass shattered on the sawdust-sprinkled boards. The smell of raw liquor smote the air like a living thing. Simmonds backed, his arms away from his sides. He saw death in the other man's eyes.

Brenner raised his free arm and wiped his face on the sleeve of his shirt. It almost seemed as if he was giving

Simmonds a chance to go for his gun. Simmonds didn't take that chance. He didn't lack guts, but he knew a gunfighting killer when he saw one.

He stopped backing as Brenner came after him. Brenner didn't halt until the muzzle of the gun was almost poking into the deputy's belly. His free hand moved downwards, lifted Simmonds' gun, let it fall with a thud to the boards. The deputy might have made a break then, bringing his hand down swiftly while Brenner was so close to him. But Simmonds was too full of overwhelming relief to think straight. Looked like he wasn't going to be gun-whipped after all.

Brenner moved away a little. 'I hear your superior officer is waiting for you somewhere,' he said. 'You better go join him. Tell him I'll probably be here when he gets back if he should want to see me.' He jerked his gun. 'Go on — move!'

Simmonds turned away from the bar, walked to the batwings, passed through them.

He let himself into the sheriff's office and got another gun from the armoury. Then, holding this in his hand, he paused. He had been tempted to go back and meet Brenner but now he realized that would be a foolish thing to do. The man would be waiting for him back there in cover in the saloon. He would have to walk back along the street alone, a perfect target.

He slid the gun into his holster and left the office, locking the door behind him. He went around the back of the jail and got on his horse and rode out of town.

He was thinking of all the things he *could* have done to turn the tables on Brenner. He was haunted by the man's lean face and killer eyes. Where had he seen them before? The memory eluded him.

He decided he had better tell old Josh about the incident. If he didn't, somebody else would. But old Josh better keep his foot out of things this time: the man called Brenner was Jay

17

Simmonds' pigeon from now on. If he stayed in Lagos — and somehow, Simmonds figured he would. Maybe Brenner had business in Lagos. A vision of the lean, somehow familiar face rose before Simmonds' eyes again. He remembered the look in those eyes and shuddered a little.

He raised his own eyes. The blue peaks shimmered in the heat-haze before him. Pretty soon he would be picking up old Josh's trail. He had to figure out just what he meant to tell the sheriff.

He pulled his hat further over his eyes to shade them from the sunglare. He began to grin. There were more ways of killing a turkey than strangling it.

★ ★ ★

The local undertaker and his assistant had taken Charlie Bennett's body away. Many folks had gone back to their interrupted siesta. Others took a drink

18

but did not get too near to the stranger. They regarded him from afar.

A young hellion all right. Things were certainly happening of late in somnolent Lagos.

Only Lemmy Dricourt had not moved. He said gruffly, 'I liked the way you handled Simmonds, son — but he'll bear watching: he's a mean cuss.'

Brenner shrugged slightly. 'Him and the sheriff chasin' somebody?' he asked.

'Yeh, coupla masked men held up the bank day 'fore yesterday. In broad daylight too. They got clean away.'

'Make a big haul?'

'No, they were a day too late. The ranch payrolls had gone out.'

Brenner's eyes shone. He might have been smiling, but his lips did not quirk.

Lemmy finished . . . 'They killed one o' the tellers though. Nervous young cuss called Billy — had never done anybody any harm.'

'Sad,' said Brenner tonelessly. 'Maybe it was the same two men who killed your friend Charlie an' took his dust to compensate a little for the lack of it here.'

Lemmy chuckled mirthlessly. 'If it was them two the sheriff an' his sidekick are shore aimin' in the wrong direction.'

'Mebbe the two men made a detour to throw the law off the scent. They could've run into old Charlie by accident.'

'Pity you didn't mention this theory to Jay Simmonds.'

'He didn't give me much chance did he?'

'No. That's Jay all over. Mebbe he means well though.'

Brenner made no answer to this. He pushed his glass across the bar to Coney for a refill. The fat saloon-keeper had caught the tail-end of the conversation. Now, as he filled Brenner's glass he said, 'Maybe we better get a posse together.'

He was not looking at Brenner but at Lemmy Dricourt. He waited for the big man's answer then, and his eyes were everywhere but upon Brenner.

Lemmy seemed to have sunk into a drunken lethargy again. But now, as he straightened up, it became evident that he had only been thinking.

'Mebbe we had at that,' he said. 'I'd shore like to get the skunk who killed old Charlie. Mebbe the two lawmen are only batting the wind an', like Brenner says, the two bank-robbers killed Charlie for his dust.'

Coney looked surprised. Evidently he hadn't heard the first part of the conversation. After a fraction of hesitation, he turned and lumbered back along the bar.

'Who's for a posse to go looking for old Charlie's murderers?' he shouted hoarsely. 'The law's off gallivanting — we gotta do what we can.'

There was a little derisive laughter. One man shouted, 'We don't need the law. I'm fer riding. It's gettin' so a man ain't safe in his own street. We gotta make an example o' somebody . . . '

'That ain't how I wanted it at all,'

growled Lemmy Dricourt to nobody in particular. 'Coney's too all-fired eager to be the centre of attraction. We want an organized posse, not a bloodlusting rabble.'

Brenner was the only one who heard him, for the turmoil was growing and shouting men were already leaving to fetch their horses. Brenner did not say anything.

3

Josh Penrose wriggled his lean buttocks over the warm rock and got once more into the shade. His bones were stiff and aching and his clothes stuck to him with sweat. He wished that old sun would quit chasing him. He was getting too old for these kind of games. He had lost count of how many times he had moved. Squinting into the glare, he stroked his grey walrus moustache absently. He didn't have any makings left and was down to the last thimbleful of water in his canteen.

He had not found any sign; all he had done was cut it. And he knew that if he went any further, Jay, smokes, water, provisions and all, was liable to lose him. He guessed he'd pick up his horse and they'd go on — though those two owl-hooters were probably way over the border by now.

Somewhere nearby a loose stone rattled. Josh's lean body straightened, tautened. All his aches and pains and his peevishness left him. His hand closed over the butt of his gun. He twisted himself gently and rose to his knees. He took out the gun.

The sound came again, nearer this time. Josh began to crawl. At the edge of the outcrop of boulders he hesitated. If he poked his head around the corner he could look down on the narrow trail from which he had climbed. He would not be able to see his horse because the beast was ground-hitched in a little boxed-in clearing where he could make a frugal meal from the brown grass. Josh wondered if the horse had been spotted.

He was reluctant to poke his head up in case he had been spotted. He had no desire to turn himself into a human turkey-shoot for some marksman. He took off his hat and hung it on his gun-barrel, elevated the gun a little, poked it around the edge of the rock.

Nothing happened.

He took the hat off the gun-barrel and put it back on his head. Then he poked his head round the rock. As he moved out of the shade the sunrays smote the side of his face like the slap of a woman's hand, something Josh had managed to steer clear of for most of his life. A voice behind him said, 'Here — you old goat.'

Josh twisted then relaxed. Jay Simmonds was grinning at him in that mocking way he had.

'What in tarnation . . . '

'I wasn't sure it was you,' interrupted the deputy. 'I had to creep up.'

'Didn't you see my horse?'

'No. I left my own horse a while back an' took to the rocks. For all I knew you might've caught up with those skunks, might've been watching 'em. I didn't mean to come riding gaily along the trail an' snarl things up.'

'Good for you, son,' said Josh with grudging admiration. He knew Jay did not like being called 'son' and it pleased him to return the younger man's half-mockery. Jay had been right in the way he had acted, however, the old lawman knew that. Jay, despite his uppishness, was a pretty good deputy.

The old man rose. 'I ain't seen hide nor hair of them two fellers. If they've come this way they've certainly been very careful not to leave any sign. I guess we better go on though. Mebbe we'll pick up something when we get out on the flat again.'

'I'll go get my horse,' said Simmonds.

They clambered down together. Josh got his own horse ready. After a few moments Jay joined him and they split the provisions up into two equal portions. Josh took a drink, rolled himself a quirly with the fresh makings.

'How about somethin' to eat?' said Jay.

'That can wait until we get out of this devils' playground.' The sheriff looked around him at the fantastic outcrops of rock, the tortured-looking vegetation.

The sun made his eyes water and he lowered them.

'It ain't safe to ride the horses even,' he complained good-humouredly. 'This rock face is the orneriest I've ever seen.'

He led the way. Both men breathed sighs of relief when, after about half-an-hour, they reached comparatively level ground. The rock was now broken up by patches of sand and stunted brown grass and pretty soon the painted desert reached out before them to a nebulous horizon shimmering in the heat-haze.

Here and there the monotonous terrain was broken by rock outcrops and clusters of cacti and other fantastic and tortured vegetation. And, even though, as the men passed over it, the scenery was of monotonous sand-grey the sun gave it, in the distance, all the colours of the rainbow and the horizon was a painted and shimmering mirage.

Josh, who had learned his tracking in the old days of the Indian wars, rode with his head bent. From time to time he dismounted from his horse and stooped to examine some tell-tale sign. Finally he said, 'Looks like they've come this way all right. I guess they took a different trail through the hills than we did. We better rest an' eat a while though I guess before we push on. This ain't an extra-wide strip of desert but we'll need everythin' we've got to get to the other side.'

'You aimin' to chase those skunks plumb into Mexico, Josh?'

'Why not? Mebbe we can drag 'em back without running foul of greaser law.'

'Or shoot it out with them.'

'Yeh, we might even have to do that.' Josh glanced quizzically at his deputy.

Presently the old man pointed and said, 'That's a large outcrop up ahead. Best shade we'll find for a long time I'm thinking. We'll rest there a mite an' have some chow.'

Jay nodded, for once saving his breath and his strength. The outcrop looked, from a distance, like one of the old covered wagons, team of six horses and all, which used to cross the plains and could still be seen sometimes. But when they reached it, it was just another outcrop, hard, craggy, uninviting and not particularly shady. They dismounted stiffly and Jay skirted the edge of the rocks looking for a place to light. He returned and Josh turned to face him and saw the change in his weatherbeaten face.

'What's bitten you? You run into a sidewinder or somethin'?'

'Come and have a look.' Jay turned on his heels. Josh followed him.

In a small patch of shade on the other side of the rock a man lay face downwards. Both men now went down on their knees, one on each side of the body.

'The buzzards haven't been at him yet,' said Jay.

'They fly high in this territory,' said Josh. 'An' they don't like the centre of the desert no more than us humans do. He ain't been here too long.' The old man looked up, shading his eyes from the sunglare. 'Looks like we've led the critturs to him.'

Jay followed the direction of his boss's gaze and saw the irregular black blobs hanging almost motionless in the yellow sky. He spat drily into the sand.

Josh rolled the body over. 'Shot in the belly,' he said. 'He didn't die very quickly or very nicely.'

The contorted unshaven face was that of a fairly young, well-made man. The contorted limbs spoke eloquently of the way he had used his strength to fight death.

'He was left here to die,' said Josh. 'His gun and belt aren't here.' He began to run his lean hands expertly over the man's clothes, through his pockets. 'Clean,' he said.

'Clean,' he repeated.

Then he gave a little exclamation and drew forth something from a pocket of the faded Levis. It was a square of black cloth.

'Hey,' said Jay Simmonds, stabbing a

finger. 'Black. Why would a man carry a black kerchief around with him — in his pocket? This *hombre*'s one of the stick-up men. Mebbe they got off with somethin' we didn't know about and fought over it . . . '

'Wait a minute-wait a minute.' Josh cut off his deputy's tirade. 'Did anybody get a good look at the two bank-robbers?'

'Only Billy the teller, maybe. An' he ain't alive any more.'

'Some of the townsfolk saw the men leaving the bank. Although they were masked there might be something about them that could be identified.' Josh rose slowly. 'There's a decision I've got to make, Jay.'

'You mean should we go after the other man, the one we figure is this one's pardner, or shall we take this one back to town an' see if we can get him identified.'

'That's it,' said Josh. 'I don't like giving up the trail but seems like we're too far behind — we might have trouble

31

in Mexico . . . ' His voice tailed off. He did not want the arrogant Jay to think him uncertain and vacillating in his old age.

'It's up to you, Josh,' said Jay. 'But I figure this is one of the bank-robbers all right.'

Josh let his hand fall with a slap to his thigh. 'So we take him back,' he said.

Jay nodded, bent towards the body. Josh was a little surprised at his side-kick's readiness to return. Not so long ago he had been rarin' to go, to get on to Mexico and maybe a shooting-match.

He helped the younger man to get the body across the front of Jay's horse, which had been fed and rested in town while the sheriff's own mount had had to make do with alkaline water and brown desert grass. After the body was secured with Jay's riata the two men rested themselves against the rock and ate a cold, frugal meal of bully-beef and biscuits washed down with water from their canteens. Afterwards they sat smoking, both, it seemed, silent with their own thoughts. Jay thought it would now be politic for him to tell his superior about the death of Charlie Bennett and about the man who called himself Tom Brenner.

Josh heard him out, only interjecting a couple of small questions. Then, when the deputy had finished, there was a pause before Josh asked:

'You ain't told it all have you, Jay? There's somethin' else in your mind.'

'You've heard it all. I didn't come out very proud on the deal I've told you that.'

'That was hard for you to tell wasn't it? But there's something else.'

'I've told it. Maybe you got somethin' in your mind, huh? You ain't ever heard of anybody called Tom Brenner have you?'

'No, cain't say I have. An' there are probably hundreds more saddle-tramps in Arizona I ain't heard of either. I'm surprised you didn't tell me about the death of old Charlie before though

— he was a friend of mine.'

'I'm sorry, maybe I should've,' said Jay. 'While we were ridin' didn't seem the right time.'

Josh gave the younger man a sidelong glance. It was not like Jay to say he was sorry about anything.

They rose and remounted their horses, set off back the way they had come. It was a silent trail. Maybe the dead weighed a little heavily now in their thoughts, particularly in those of the sheriff, who had lost an old friend. Charlie's visits to town, his kindness, his independence, his orneriness, his habit of shooting-up one saloon or another from time to time was going to be missed by a good many people in Lagos. His killer ought to swing high. Swinging was too good for him. He ought to die slowly.

Evil seemed to have burst wholesale over Lagos in the last few days. Death had come swiftly. Young Billy, the teller; Charlie; and now this stranger who could be one of the bank-robbers.

These were not saloon brawls, death dealt swiftly in the heat of argument. There was something more evil about them. And now there was another stranger in town. A hard-bitten younker, probably a killer — or, at least, that was what Jay said.

Whatever he was he must be quite a bobcat, the sheriff reflected, to have twisted the arrogant deputy's tail the way he'd done. Maybe Jay had acted too precipitately in the way he had approached the stranger; and, then again, maybe he hadn't. Josh figured he would not like to commit himself to an opinion until he had met this Tom Brenner himself.

4

It was night when the sheriff, his deputy and their silent passenger reached Lagos. By this time the various honky-tonks and suchlike establishments should have been jumping. But there were not many lights, and main street was strangely silent.

They only passed one man, who turned to stare after them and the recumbent passenger across the front of Simmonds' saddle. They dismounted in front of the sheriff's office and jailhouse. Josh unlocked the door and opened it. Jay cradled the body in his arms, carried it into the office and laid it on the battered couch beneath the window.

The silence was oppressive. No clankety piano, no distant voice raised in song. The two men exchanged glances. 'Let's go see what ails this

36

town,' said Josh and led the way.

First of all they took their horses into the small stable which adjoined the jail. They unsaddled the beasts and saw that they had plenty of oats and water. Then they moved side by side down the boardwalk, their bootheels clattering in the stillness.

They entered Coney's saloon, the biggest establishment of its kind in Lagos, the hive of gossip when anything untoward occurred. There were only five men in the place and two of those were on the business side of the bar. Coney was nowhere to be seen: the couple were his relief barman, a crippled youth named Caspar and a harelipped oldster known as Happy Cal. He was not a natural harelip, but had been made that way by a blow from an Indian scalping knife. His mouth was twisted into a perpetual grin. He opened it wider now as he saw the two new arrivals.

'The law's arrived at last,' he chortled.

The two officers looked around at the assembled company. They were a decrepit bunch. Three percentage girls sat at a table playing cards. The company this evening was evidently not much to their liking either.

Happy Cal pushed a bottle of rye and two glasses across the bar. The sheriff lifted the bottle mechanically. 'What's been goin' on?' he asked.

'You're about three hours too late to lead the posse, Josh,' chortled Cal.

'What posse?'

'The one that's gone out after the killers of pore ol' Charlie Bennett.'

'I know about Charlie — Jay told me. D'you mean they've got a line on the killers?'

Cal looked uncertain. Caspar limped forward, put in, 'Naw, they had no line. They just went out playin' vigilante.'

'How many?'

'About every able-bodied man in town I guess,' Caspar's tone was bitter. Josh realized, with a spasm of pity, that, despite his sneers, the crippled youth would have liked to be with that bunch.

'Who led 'em?'

'Coney — Lemmy Dricourt . . . '

'Where's that stranger who found Charlie?' put in Jay Simmonds harshly.

'He went with them too. He had to show 'em where he had found Charlie.'

Jay turned towards his superior officer. 'Mebbe we better go after 'em, huh, Josh?'

'We'll wait awhile,' said the sheriff. 'They'll probably come back empty-handed.'

'They'll come back empty-handed all right,' grinned Happy Cal. But it was obvious he did not mean it in the same way as the sheriff did.

Josh frowned. His walrus moustache gave him a horsey look.

Young Caspar said, 'That stranger — Tom Brenner he calls himself — has a kind of a theory.'

Both lawmen looked mighty interested. Caspar went on, 'He thinks the two masked men who stuck up the bank met Charlie an' killed him for his dust.'

The two lawmen exchanged glances. Jay opened his mouth. Then something in the sheriff's eyes warned him and he began to take an interest in his drink, taking it down in one gulp. The sheriff followed his example then said, 'So-long.' Jay followed him from the saloon.

As they hit the boardwalk Josh asked, 'Whereabouts was Charlie Bennett's body found?'

'I'm not sure. But I'm pretty certain it wasn't anywhere near the territory we've covered. Our corpse's pardner would've had to work fast if . . . '

'But we're not sure our corpse was one of the bank-robbers,' put in Josh.

'There seems little doubt. That black kerchief . . . ' Jay left his sentence unfinished as they reached the office and passed inside.

'First thing I'm going to do is have a good cleanup. Then I'm going to cook a man-sized meal. You'll stay for supper, Jay?'

The older man's imperturbility always irked Simmonds. But this time he held his peace. 'Sure,' he said. 'Sure, Josh.'

'Go an' get the undertaker, Jay. Bring him down to the office.'

'Sure, Josh.'

The deputy left the office. Josh heard the heavy bootheels clattering purposefully away and smiled at some secret joke as he passed into the back room. He was wiping lather from his face when he heard Jay return, somebody else's footsteps joining the deputy's. Josh strode to the middle door and hastily wiped himself clean as he saw the visitor was a woman.

'Evening, Miss Louise.'

'Evening, Sheriff. My father and his assistant have gone out with the posse. I came along to see if there was anything I could do.' Her dark eyes flickered toward the still form on the couch. She showed no evidence of emotion.

Josh said, 'It was very good of you to be so thoughtful, Louise. But I figure this is man's work. He'll — it'll keep till your father gets back.'

The girl inclined her dark sleek head,

the heartshaped face. 'Just as you say, Mr Penrose.'

Jay Simmonds looked down on the girl from his superior height. She was a little below the average for a woman, lithe and neat and gently sensuous in her white shirt-waist, tan skirt and short embroidered vest.

Jay said, 'That's the first time I've ever known Bern Cantell to go out with a posse.'

'Father is a man of peace,' said Louise 'But old Mr Bennett was his friend. Father could not stay at home while there was any chance of Mr Bennett's murderer being caught.'

'Did your father think the posse really had a line on old Charlie's killer?' asked the sheriff.

The girl looked a little puzzled. 'Yes, I suppose so. And he wanted to see justice done.'

'Bern doesn't believe in lynch-law,' said Josh softly.

The girl shook her head, her face sober. 'They were a rabble . . . '

As the girl's voice trailed off, Josh let his hand fall with a little slap to his thigh, always a signal of decision with him. 'Take Louise home, Jay,' he said. 'We're going after that posse.'

'Sure, Josh,' said the deputy with alacrity.

The girl's face dimpled as she put in, 'I'll be all right. I'm quite capable of walking down the street on my lonesome.'

Jay looked a little peeved as he escorted her to the door. But he brightened as, on returning, he saw Josh buckling on his gunbelt. The deputy followed suit and they went out to their horses, saddled them up and rode out of town.

'Supper will have to wait,' said old Josh grimly. 'Have a biscuit.' He handed the bag over to his sidekick. They had been out about two hours and it must have been getting late, when they heard the drumming of hooves up ahead, the sound coming nearer. Josh led the way cautiously off the trail, where the two men held their horses motionless in the meagre shadows of desert trees.

The riders seemed to be slowing down. The sound of voices came next; it appeared there was some kind of argument going on.

'Mebbe they heard us,' murmured Jay.

'No, I figure they were making too much noise themselves . . . Careful.' The sheriff added the last word as he saw his deputy draw his gun.

The riders came out of the darkness. 'It's them all right,' said Jay.

'Listen,' hissed the sheriff.

A single voice, the fat, phlegm-burbling voice of Coney, rose above all else. 'Well, where's he come from? Let him . . . '

The deep voice of Lemmy Dricourt broke in, but his words were indistinguishable. These two men were in the front rank. A third rode between them.

'That's the stranger I told you about,' said Jay. 'The one in the middle.'

'Mebbe it's him that Lemmy and

Coney are arguing about,' said Josh. 'Though it don't seem to be fazing him none — he's riding like there's nobody else around.'

'He's a cool and cunning customer,' said Jay.

Josh kneed his horse forward on to the trail. The bunch of riders swelled, scattered a little. Then Coney said, 'It's the sheriff.'

With Jay riding behind him, the old lawman rode forward. The bunch reined in. The sheriff's voice rang out curtly in the sudden stillness.

'Well — did you lynch anybody?'

'We didn't even see anybody,' said Lemmy Dricourt. 'Not even a jack-rabbit between here and the hills. An' no tracks either.'

'I tell yuh . . . ' began Coney.

'Shut up!' Lemmy's voice was harsh, laden with menace. When he was sober the flabby Herculean blacksmith was a human grizzly.

Coney left the rest of his sentence unspoken and kept his mouth shut.

'We'll ride back to town with you,' said the sheriff, very mildly now. He fell into line in the front rank. Jay Simmonds followed his example.

'Let's go,' said old Josh, looking straight ahead.

Bernard Cantell, the lean undertaker with the gentle face, rode almost directly behind the elder lawman. But it was not until the lights of Lagos came into sight that Josh turned and said, 'We've got another customer for you, Bern.'

'I hope it's not another friend of mine,' said Cantell in his deep, gentle voice.

'No, it's a stranger.'

The arrival of the law and Josh's quiet authority had had a sobering effect on the posse. But now, as the sheriff's words were heard by those in the front ranks, a babble of voices broke out.

Questions were flung at the sheriff. He answered none of them, watching out of the corner of his eye the lean, dark young man who rode beside him. Since saying 'Howdy, Sheriff' at their meeting, Tom Brenner had not spoken another word. Even now he acted as if he was riding alone. Josh figured he was a man who was pretty used to riding alone.

Still disregarding the questions, the sheriff, followed by Jay Simmonds and Bern Cantell, quitted the bunch outside Coney's place. Looking back, he saw Tom Brenner enter the saloon with the rest of them. The sheriff caught his deputy looking back, too. They exchanged glances but neither of them spoke.

Bern Cantell was also looking back, but for a different reason. His assistant had endeavoured to lose himself in the crowd entering the saloon. But the gentle undertaker spotted him and made a sign and the gangling youth on the rawboned nag came reluctantly after them.

The four men entered the office and undertaker and assistant made a professional examination of the corpse.

'Go fetch a basket, Mack,' said Cantell presently.

The youth shambled away, returning a few minutes later dragging a long wickerwork basket. 'Some of the fellers spotted me an' followed,' he said.

'They won't be able to see anything,' said Cantell.

The two of them lifted the body into the basket and carted it away. Questions were flung at them in the street, but the only replies that were given were by shrugs of Cantell's lean shoulders.

The sheriff took off his gunbelt, hung it over the back of a chair. 'Now for that supper,' he said, and passed into the kitchen.

Jay Simmonds seemed as if he would call after him, but evidently thought better of it. And when the old man called him to come and make coffee, he went almost meekly into the kitchen.

5

They were sitting eating at the deal table, when they heard the office door open. Simmonds took his gun from beside his plate and rose and went outside. A few seconds later the sheriff heard his voice, coming a little harshly, another voice answering it. The old man rose, passed through the middle door.

The two young men were standing facing each other like bristling terriers.

'What can I do for you, son?' asked Josh.

Tom Brenner turned his head slightly to face the sheriff. 'I've got something I want to show you,' he said. 'It's something I found by the body of the old man.'

'Have you showed it to anybody else?'

'I didn't get a chance to. Anyway, I figured you were the man who ought to see it first. It might be a clue or somethin'.'

'All right, Jay — relax,' said the sheriff.

Simmonds scowled, tucked his gun into the top of his pants and moved over to the desk. From beneath the yellow lamp he stood glowering at Brenner.

Brenner dug deep into the pocket of his chaps and brought forth a piece of black cloth. He shook it out. 'It was beneath the old man's body,' he said.

The sheriff took the cloth from him and carried it nearer to the light. 'There's blood on it.'

'The old man's blood,' said Brenner. 'But somehow I didn't figure it was his kerchief. He already had one round his neck. A purty gaily-coloured one it had once been. I didn't figure he was the sort of old jasper who'd go for black.'

'He didn't,' said Josh, half to himself. 'He liked the colours of the desert at sun-up an' sunset. He liked the saloons an' the colour of the girls' dresses an' playing cards and roulette wheels, he liked the colour of life far more than he did that yellow stuff he was always seeking. Every man's got to search for something, I guess. It ain't the thing itself, it's what it stands for . . . '

Josh's voice tailed off. Brenner eyed him gravely, not seeming to see anything strange in a hardbitten old Western lawman talking that way. But maybe Jay Simmonds had not been listening at all, for he broke in harshly now with, 'That was a damned smart move that was — a *damned* smart move!'

Brenner turned slowly. 'You keep crowding me,' he said. 'What's biting you now?'

'Nobody saw hide nor hair of old Charlie's killer. Or any tracks — except your own, no doubt. It's very convenient to blame a man in a black kerchief, one of the men who held up the bank. And how could you have got the black kerchief? There's only one way . . . '

'You sneaking skunk!' Brenner's voice slashed across the room.

'Hold it,' said the sheriff. But he had no gun to back up his command.

Only a levelled gun in somebody else's hand could have stopped these two. And there was no gun in anybody else's hand, the sheriff's belt was over a chair well out of his reach. The only available guns were in the belts of the two hotheaded young men.

Like a man approaching a sputtering fuse, the sheriff began to move in between them. But he was not fast enough. 'Nobody calls me . . . ' said Simmonds. He did not finish his sentence. His movement was a flurry. The bark of the gun was deafening in the enclosed space.

Simmonds gave a harsh cry of pain as his weapon clattered to the boards. The heavy slug had spun him around. He hung over the desk, retching a little as he clutched his wounded arm.

The sheriff had a split-second in which to move and he took every advantage of it. He scooped the paper-weight off the edge of the desk and flung it, all in one sweeping movement. The paperweight was of solid brass, made into the shape of a wide-brimmed ornamented sombrero, a relic of a pillaging raid into Mexico when Josh was a hot-blooded youth. It caught Brenner on the side of the head and he went down, his gun skittling along the floor to within a yard of the sheriff's feet.

Josh bent and picked up the gun, and when Brenner climbed dazedly to his feet, he found himself covered. Bootheels hammered on the board-walk outside. The door was flung open and Mack, the undertaker's assistant, looked in.

'We don't need you yet, son,' said Josh with grim humour. 'But you can go and fetch the doc, if you will.'

Mack bobbed his head and withdrew. His heavy steps faded away, but others took up the refrain.

Josh backed across the room and

turned the key on the inside of the office door. He jerked the gun. 'Go over to that door opposite. Open it and go through.'

Brenner stood his ground. 'What are you aiming to do?'

'I'm going to lock you up. You almost killed my deputy.'

'I could've killed him. I could've plugged him dead centre. Anyway, he went for his gun first — it was self-defence. If I'd let him get away with it, I'd be a dead man now.

This was no tirade. This was unemotional facts told in a flat, toneless voice. But the sheriff said, 'Do as you're told, son,' and his voice was like ice.

Brenner marched over to the door, opened it and passed through into the cell block.

'You can't keep me here,' he said, as if those words were his final words.

'I figure you'll be safer here anyway,' said the sheriff cryptically.

'You don't mean . . . ' Brenner left his sentence unfinished, merely shrugged his shoulders.

He did not say anything else at all, but when he turned after being locked in the cell there was something in his eyes that the sheriff did not like.

Somebody was hammering on the outer door. 'Open up,' yelled a voice. 'It's me — Limpole.'

Josh unlocked the door. 'Come on in, doc.' He ignored the questions of the mob which had gathered outside, shutting the door in their faces. The tall, stooping medico wore his grey hair long in old Frontier style. He crossed to Jay Simmonds who was still leaning over the desk, cursing to himself.

'Why didn't you sit down, man?' snapped the doctor. 'Here — come over to this couch.'

Finally Simmonds was reposed upon the couch beneath the window, the couch which had a short while ago held the body of the mysterious stranger.

'Just a flesh wound,' pronounced the doctor. 'But you've lost a lot of blood.'

'My gun-arm . . . '

'Your gun-arm will be as good as new in a couple of weeks, though I can't see that it will be any credit to you. Who did this?'

In a few words the sheriff told him. The doctor had no comment to make. He stabbed a finger at Simmonds. 'Don't let this loco young coot go on the rampage again.'

'I'll watch him,' promised the sheriff.

The doctor finished dressing the shallow wound near Simmonds' bicep. Then the sheriff let Limpole out before returning to the deputy.

'I'll kill him,' Simmonds was muttering. 'I'll kill him.'

'You can get that idea out of your head right away,' said Josh curtly.

Simmonds looked up at him. 'It's plain. Plain as turkey tracks. He's the other bank-robber. The two of 'em met old Charlie and killed him then made a detour to throw us off the scent. Then they had a quarrel over Charlie's dust an' Brenner, or whatever his name is, killed his pardner. Then he went and picked up Charlie's body and carried it here, to throw suspicion away from himself, figuring nobody would suspect him of being one of the bank robbers, or the killer, if he came in so boldly.'

'He was taking a big risk. Somebody might've recognized him.'

'No, not so big, I don't think. The only one who might have recognized him was Billy, the teller, an' they'd made sure he would never talk again.'

'His limp! Wouldn't somebody have spotted his limp?'

'Those two buzzards left their horses right outside the bank. They only had to cross the sidewalk to make their getaway. In that short while people wouldn't be able to notice the limp. Anyway, there was nobody right near. There were only two more men in the bank besides Billy and they were way back; they only saw the tail-end of the bandits, then they ran to see what they could do for Billy.

'There's another factor Brenner could cleverly take into consideration, too — people were thinking of *two* men, not just one. That's where the black kerchief comes in. His *own* kerchief — he'd probably been carrying it in his pocket all the time — if he pretended he'd found it by Charlie's body, proof that the two hold-up men had done the killing, he, as one man, would not be sus-pected . . . '

'You're a good detective, Jay,' said the sheriff. 'You've got a good case there. But it has its flaws — quite a few of them.'

'You sound as if you're on his side!'

'A lawman has to look at both sides. It's time you learned that.'

'He gave himself away! Look at the way he acted when I called him out.'

'You threw down on him, you mean. I guess he had plenty of provocation.'

'He meant to kill me. I could see it in his eyes. He's a born killer.'

Josh made no comment on this at all. Maybe the younker was a killer. He was certainly a fast shooter. Jay was fast, but against Brenner he had seemed a novice — and Jay knew it; no wonder he wanted to see a rope around Brenner's neck.

On the other hand, Josh chided himself, maybe he was being a little hard on his hot-tempered deputy, tightening those old reins again a mite too quickly. Jay had a case against Brenner all right. The younker could be a cunning one, a deadly one: Josh remembered how he had looked, back there in that cell. Producing the black kerchief as proof that the bank-robbers had killed Charlie Bennett, when all the time he knew the second bank-robber was lying dead in the middle of the desert, would be a really clever move.

But there was the time factor! Josh looked at his assistant and said:

'How do you account for the fact that, if Brenner did both killings, Charlie's body and the body of the other man were so far apart — almost in opposite directions, in fact?'

'I've been thinking about that,' said

Simmonds. 'Maybe Brenner killed his pardner before he killed Charlie. They had a quarrel — a gunfight. Brenner left the body there and, figuring maybe he was being followed, made a detour. Then he ran into Charlie, killed him an' robbed him and calmly carried the body into town. He said he heard shots, but he didn't see anybody. That doesn't ring true. If there was anybody else, surely there would have been signs of some kind, surely the posse would've picked up the trail.'

'It was dark when they got to the spot.'

'How did Brenner know about the bandits if . . . '

'I guess Lemmy or Coney told him.'

'He could've produced the black kerchief then. Why didn't he? Because he thought it would incriminate him. But he had time to think afterwards and he figured it would be a real smart move if he gave you the kerchief with an appropriate tale. Making believe he had *kept* it for you. That's likely, isn't it?

Leading the posse, too. The spot he took 'em to might not have been anywhere near where Charlie was killed.'

The sheriff shook his head from side to side. 'You make a good case against him. But there's no real proof. We need proof.'

'I wonder if he knows we've found his dead pardner.'

'He must've heard me tell Bern Cantell, he was riding right the side of me. I guess he could surmise the rest.'

'Yeh, an' mebbe that's another reason why he came here: to try an' make sure. But Bern and Mack had taken the body away and beaten him to it. But he soon found a good excuse for visiting — the kerchief. There's another thing, Josh.' Simmonds' voice was very earnest now. 'I got an idea I've seen Brenner someplace before. I don't imagine for a moment that his name is really Brenner. Mebbe I've seen his face on a photo . . . '

'On a dodger you mean?'

'Yes, wouldn't it be a good idea to look through all the back numbers we've got.'

Josh shrugged. 'All right.' He crossed to the desk, opened the wide drawer, took out a thick sheaf of bills. He laid them out on the desk and Simmonds came across.

The two men began to scan through the bills. Wanted notices; some of them from as far back as ten years ago; some of them had hung on walls until they were yellow and fly-specked. Some of the faces were those of men long since dead, violently in most cases, from a lawman's bullet or a hemp necktie. Some of them, as far as these border officials knew, had never been caught or, at least, had met justice in some other area of the wide South-West.

Most of the faces were young or middle-aged. Hard, vicious; but in some cases, even likeable. There was no set pattern for Western desperadoes: many of them were just high-spirited young cowhands gone wrong. There were faces that looked something like Tom Brenner's, but none that could actually be identified as this. There were notorious names; names that would go down in history and be coloured by legend and by the pens of unscrupulous romancers: many a cold-blooded murderer was to become a Robin Hood of the West, his once dreaded name a song on the lips of little children.

But there was no name, 'Tom Brenner.'

Simmonds gave an exclamation of disgust. He said, 'Don't think I'm tryin' to railroad the man. But he ain't acted right. When we were back on the trail, remember — we heard something. Seems like Coney ain't happy about this Brenner *hombre* either.'

'We can only surmise that,' said Josh. 'I've got some more dodgers in the back place.' He crossed to the middle door and passed through it.

He returned a few seconds later and spread a few more bills out on the desk. 'These are more recent ones.'

Simmonds skimmed through them quickly; stopped. 'This one! This looks like Brenner! I remember this — we got it about twelve months ago.' Simmonds ran his finger along the lines of print beneath the black and white picture. He read aloud, his voice rising:

'Len Santos, age twenty-three . . . five feet eleven . . . hundred and seventy pounds . . . wanted for murder and bank-robbery in Calvarez County . . . five-hundred dollars reward . . . '

'I guess the description could fit Brenner all right,' put in the sheriff. 'An' a few other thousand rannies. An' the picture could fit any dark lean-faced younker — if it comes to that, even a yaller-haired man could look dark on a photo like that one.'

Simmonds could not argue about that: the picture was a very poor one. 'Bank-robbery an' murder,' he muttered. 'I wish I could remember where I've seen that Brenner before.' Then his voice rose again. 'Hell, this is gettin' us nowhere, an' this goddamned arm o' mine is givin' me gyp. I'm goin' home to bed.'

He turned away. Over his shoulder he said, 'See you in the mornin', old-timer. If you should want me before then though, let me know.'

'Sure. Goodnight, Jay.'

'Goodnight.'

The sound of Simmonds' clattering bootheels died away into the night. Old Josh looked a little grimly at the closed door. Simmonds lodged with an old widow woman at the other end of town. To get there he had to pass Coney's place. Josh figured that Jay wouldn't be too tired or too agonized to drop into the saloon for a drink. Jay occasionally drowned his peevishness in drink and, once he was inebriated, he was everybody's friend and talked like a blue streak.

But . . . Josh shook his head from side to side: he was not his deputy's keeper!

He did not dislike Jay Simmonds. The boy had guts, and the makings of a good lawman, if his pugnacity did not earn him an early and violent death. His uppishness irritated Josh. But, above all, the old man wanted to be fair. Justice and fairness was his creed. Maybe he was misjudging Jay again, maybe the younker *would* go right past the saloon, and so to bed.

The old man went into the kitchen and heated up some more coffee. He poured a large mug full of the thickish, steaming liquid. On a plate he arrayed a pile of corncake biscuits. He put the lot on a small tin-tray and carried it through to the cell-block, adding his gun to the collection, too, as he passed through the office.

Tom Brenner was sitting, smoking, on the bunk beneath the barred window. He looked up. Josh lowered the tray gently to the floor, took the gun from it, levelled the business-end of the weapon at the prisoner.

'Stay where you are, son.'

Brenner did not move, just watched with those strange smouldering eyes.

66

Josh angled the cup through the bars first, then pushed the tray beneath them. 'Put the stuff back through into the passage when you've finished with it.'

'How long you aiming to keep me here, sheriff?'

'That depends,' said Josh. Then he added, cryptically, 'You behave yourself an' you'll be all right.' He was not quite sure himself of what he meant by that.

'What's the charge?'

'Disturbin' the peace.'

'That'll hold me I guess until you an' your fancy deputy cook up somethin' else,' said Brenner. 'I had figured you for a different man.'

Josh had nothing to say to that. He turned away. But, as he entered the office, he was fingering his walrus moustache, a sure sign that he was disturbed and puzzled.

6

When Jay Simmonds had said he was not trying to 'railroad' Tom Brenner he was, by his lights, speaking the truth. He would not exactly object to seeing Brenner swinging at the end of a rope or, better still, going down before his (Simmonds') gun-blast. But he figured either method would all be in the way of justice.

The evidence, such as it was, had led him to believe — and he would not admit that he *wanted* to believe it — that Brenner was a bank-robber and at least a double-murderer. Had the sheriff of Lagos been any other than Josh Penrose, Simmonds figured Brenner would be in jail on a charge of murder, instead of just assault, or whatever it was. Simmonds considered that old Josh carried his sense of fairness too far at times. He wanted to prove to the old goat that this time he was wrong — badly wrong.

Simmonds figured he was no slouch — even Josh had said he was a good detective. Well, he'd do some detecting on his lonesome now, and build up a real cast-iron case against Tom Brenner.

With this in mind, he entered Coney's place. He could not see Coney right away, but he spotted Lemmy Dricourt in his usual position against the bar and crossed the floor towards him.

The place was packed and there was a deafening babble of voices, broken at intervals by the clanking of the piano and banjo in the corner, a snatch of song, the squeal of a playful percentage girl. Every table was full and the taro and the chuck-a-luck layouts were booming. The air was full of blue smoke and redolent of liquor, tobacco, cheap scent, horses and indifferently-washed humanity. Greetings and questions were thrown at Simmonds and his bandaged arm. He ignored all alike, wending his way through the shuffling dancers that filled the small piece of floor cleared for the purpose. He reached Lemmy Dricourt's side and greeted him.

The sagging Hercules straightened up and regarded him with bleary eyes. He made a flourish with one huge hand.

'The law arrives,' he boomed. 'And with flag still flying, too. You got hurt, huh, Jay? You got shot mebbe. I'd figured it might be you. Did Tom Brenner do it, Jay?'

Simmonds managed with difficulty to control his temper. As heads were turned his way he acted like a man humouring a drunkard. 'Have a drink, Lemmy,' he said.

'Thanks, Jay. Rye.'

Simmonds called for two ryes. The crippled youth, Caspar, served them. Simmonds asked him where Coney was. Caspar said Coney was having supper, but would be back in soon. It was late — looked like there would be an all-night session.

Over their drinks, Simmonds told Lemmy Dricourt of the incident in the sheriff's office. The black scarf; Brenner's rage at being confronted with the deputy's suspicion.

'He threw down on me,' said Simmonds. 'I didn't have a chance. I think he meant to kill me.'

'He ain't exactly your bosom friend,' said Lemmy. 'An' now Josh has clapped him in jail, huh? On what charge?'

'Wal, you know Josh. He must be fair. But I don't think there's much doubt in his mind now that Brenner is the man we want.'

'If that's the case, he certainly took a chance in bringing that black kerchief to the office, didn't he?'

'Like I told yuh, that was his devilish cunning. An' he might have got away with it if I hadn't been there.'

Simmonds called for another couple of drinks. Then he asked, 'Who told Brenner about the bank-robbery?'

Lemmy had the faculty of becoming

sober in an instant, no matter how much liquor he had imbibed. Now he wrinkled his brow; then said, 'I told him.'

'An' what did he say?'

'He said mebbe it was the same two men who had killed Charlie Bennett.'

'I figured that might be the way it was,' said Simmonds, triumphantly. 'That must've been when he started to think out his little scheme. He didn't produce the black scarf then, did he?'

'No-o.'

'No, he wouldn't. He was saving it for a smarter move. But it didn't work. I'll see . . . ' Simmonds' voice had been rising. Now he lowered it as Coney put in an appearance.

'What's biting you?' said the saloon keeper flatly.

Simmonds called for three drinks this time. He knew he had an ally in Coney. Subsequent conversation proved his surmise to be correct. The three men went on drinking.

Simmonds was keeping pace with

two seasoned topers. He had not meant to get drunk. But it was inevitable. And when he was drunk he began to show off and talk in a loud voice.

More and more people were drawn into the discussion, as the lawman acclaimed, over and over, that he would 'have justice!'

Coney, despite Lemmy Dricourt's grumbled protests, backed the deputy up. After all, wasn't it the duty of every right-thinking man to be on the side of the law. And, pretty soon, other drink-inflamed men — and the saloon was pretty full of them — were raving about justice. How could folks get justice, punish thieves and murderers, if their town was ramrodded by a doddering old goat of a sheriff who couldn't make up his own mind about anything? Simmonds had not said this — in his way, he was loyal to old Josh — but in the liquor-soaked heat of the moment, he had probably more than once implied it.

Pretty soon, too, men were streaming

towards the batwings, spilling out on to the boardwalk, all the time yelling for justice.

Lemmy Dricourt caught hold of Simmonds by the shoulders and shook him.

'Now look what you've done, you drunken fool!'

'Who are you calling drunk? You . . . Take your hands off me!'

'You're a baby,' snarled Lemmy. 'I've drunk twice as much as you. Call yourself a lawman! You're a disgrace to the profession. You've got no more guts than a jack-rabbit.'

Lemmy's rage got the better of him, and he gave the deputy a ringing slap across the side of the head, sending him staggering. Jay went for his gun, then almost screamed with agony as his wounded arm made itself felt.

Lemmy had contemptuously turned his back on him and, shouting something that the deputy could not hear, was moving after the mob. Simmonds saw Coney's bobbing fat figure, too.

But the saloon keeper did not seem to be trying to stop anything.

The blow Lemmy had given him had sobered Jay somewhat. He remembered old Josh alone at the jail and he began to get scared. He knew the old man's courage, the way he would face that mob, doing his duty to the bitter end.

The deputy was galvanized into action. He flung himself into the van of the mob, going past Lemmy like a whirlwind. 'Wait a minute. This ain't the way to do it!'

For a moment, he had forgotten his wounded arm. Now, as he was jostled on all sides, the injured member began to get knocked. Pain screamed through his body, upset his liquor-soaked belly. He began to feel sick. The room, the yellow lights, the yammering faces began to spin around him.

A harder blow smote the wound. He began to retch, falling. A boot caught him on the side of the head and he knew no more.

★ ★ ★

Josh Penrose's worst fears were realized when he heard the ominous booming. This was not, by far, the first bloodlusting mob he had heard, but, if he lived to be a hundred and fifty and the West became bathed in blood, he would never get used to that sound.

He had a short spasm of panic, as any man might have done. He had never considered himself to be a brave man: he only did things as he saw them and, whenever possible, without deviation. Now he forgot fear as he buckled on his gunbelt, tucked a spare gun into his waistband, took a shotgun from the armoury rack, too. He dodged outside and closed the shutters over the windows He could see the nebulous mass of the mob as they passed through rays of yellow light. He was relieved that nobody yet had lit the traditional flaming torches.

He went back into the office and locked and bolted the door behind him.

He heard the man in the cell-block yell: maybe the younker was getting scared. Josh went through. But Tom Brenner did not look scared, just a little grim, that was all.

'Does that noise mean what I think it means, sheriff?'

'I'm afraid it does, son. But don't worry — I can handle things.'

Brenner's lips curled thinly. 'You're old enough to know you can never be sure of anything, of what you can handle or what you can't handle. Give me a couple of guns and let me loose out there.'

'An' you'd shoot 'em all, huh? Now you're talking a damn sight sillier than I was.'

Josh turned on his heels and went back into the office.

The noise of the crowd, like the baying of hundreds of hungry wolves, sounded nearer. Josh picked up his shotgun and crossed the room. He kneeled on the couch beneath the window. He unhitched one wing of the window and threw it back, so that the bare boards of the shutter were revealed, complete with two loopholes, one above the other. He pressed his eye to one slit and poked the muzzle of the gun against the other.

The crowd suddenly surged into view, began to swell and mass in front of the office. A few of the bolder characters climbed on to the board-walk.

Josh elevated the muzzle of his gun a little and pressed the trigger. He was in a funny position and the recoil almost knocked him over. The charge screamed over the heads of the crowd. In a second the boardwalk was as clear as if it had been swept by a hurricane. The crowd swelled and jittered. There were startled shouts; and angry ones. Then the noise died as folks awaited the speech they were sure the sheriff was going to make. The shot had been the signal. Now the words came. They were few; and to the point.

'Go back to your homes, you fools,

before somebody gets hurt!'

The sheriff scanned as many of the faces as he could see in the half light. He was relieved to find that Jay Simmonds was not in the front ranks, that Jay hadn't got crazy drunk and led the mob here. If the crowd lacked a leader maybe he could handle them. But his hopes were dashed when he saw Coney push his way to the front of the crowd. Coney's presence carried weight, in more ways than one. Despite his front of flabby good-humour, Coney could be a real mean one.

Now the fat man shouted in his husky burbling voice, 'We don't mean you any harm, Josh, you know that! But we want the man who killed old Charlie Bennett!'

Angry cries backed up Coney's short speech. The crowd was glad to have a leader into whose mind they could sink their own minds, until they became one huge blind mob, a mob mind.

Josh waited until the noise had died again then he shouted, 'You've come to the wrong place, gentlemen.' Hardly were the words out of his mouth when somebody bawled, 'Don't stall. We know you've got him in there — that Brenner *hombre*!'

'Yeh . . . We want Brenner . . .'

Coney waved his fat arms. 'Open that door, Josh, an' let us in. Nobody'll harm you — but if you get in our way . . .'

He left his sentence unfinished. But the crowd ended it for him, with a threatening roar. It was like the roar of a pack of wild beasts. It shocked Josh into involuntary action. He let off the gun again.

The crowd eddied and swirled. Coney shook his fist. That charge had almost torn a groove across his balding pate . . . But nothing was funny — this was bloody action. The roaring crowd surged forward. As those at the back pressed forward, Coney, and a few more with him, was shoved on to the boardwalk.

Maybe they did not think the sheriff

would loose a blast into the midst of them. Josh himself knew he couldn't do that, although, in protecting State property, he had every reason to do so. But he was not, and never had been, a licensed killer.

Things were getting desperate. Again Josh had a spasm of panic. Fear, too; but fear not wholly for himself. He took the gun away from the loophole. A stone clattered on the shutters, another on the door. He swung the gun towards the door as he got down from the couch. He stood irresolute for a moment of time, then crossed the office and passed into the cell-block.

'Well, sheriff,' said Tom Brenner. 'Are you gonna throw me to the wolves?'

His voice was no longer toneless. It held a strange emotion, a note of sardonic humour, which surprised Josh Penrose. He said:

'You got a lot to learn, son.' With the shotgun cradled in the crook of his arm and his finger on the trigger, he unlocked the cell-door with his other hand. Then he backed across the passage.

'Go out the back way,' he ordered curtly.

'Run away you mean? Admit the guilt of whatever you an' that mob think I've done?'

'Don't be a fool. Hurry up before they take it into their crazy heads to surround the joint.'

'Give me a gun.'

'I wouldn't trust you that far, son. But I ain't sure about you, an' I don't want your blood on my head, so I'm giving you a chance to escape. Get moving before I lose my patience an' this shotgun goes off.'

The old man's voice was metallic now. Brenner did not argue any longer but allowed himself to be shepherded to the back door and through it. The sheriff watched him dissolve into the darkness before closing the door and going back down the passage. Therefore he did not see the figures who approached Brenner from the alley that ran along the side of the jail.

Looked like some smart alecs had already begun to surround the place.

7

The noise from outside had undergone a subtle change. Peeping through the loopholes again, Sheriff Penrose learned the reason for this. There were more people on the boardwalk, but they had their backs to the office. Josh felt a surge of relief as he recognized Jay Simmonds and Lemmy Dricourt.

He went to the office door and unlocked it and, shotgun at the ready, stepped out.

A roar greeted him. The crowd surged, quietened. On the boardwalk, facing the mob with levelled guns, stood four men. Simmonds, Dricourt, and besides, Coney's two relief barmen, Happy Cal, the harelipped oldster, and Caspar, the crippled youth. Coney did not seem very pleased about this arrangement, but, as Happy Cal had got a gun-muzzle within a few inches of his erstwhile employer's enormous belly, there was not much the saloon-owner could do.

'I was gettin' sick o' that job anyway,' chortled Cal. His pardner, Caspar, stood next to him. The crippled younker had a huge Frontier-model Colt in each hand. Frail and lopsided though he was, he looked dangerous. There was the light of an unholy glee in his pale eyes. Lemmy Dricourt was as huge, stooping and phlegmatic as ever, but his companion, Jay Simmonds, was a sight to set a strong man screaming. He had lost his hat and his hair was unkempt and one side of his head was plastered with drying blood, which had sent grotesque red trails down his pallid cheeks. His lips were drawn back from his teeth in a wolfish snarl and his eyes blazed.

Josh moved between his deputy and Dricourt. The crowd were at bay. Somebody in the front might do something rash or be skittled forward by those in the back. Josh did not want his hot-tempered deputy to kill anybody if it could possibly be avoided.

But action, when it came, exploded further along the boardwalk.

A man called hoarsely, 'Get back, you gimpy little skunk!' and lashed out at young Caspar with a gun.

One of the younker's Colts bucked and flamed. The man screamed and clutched his stomach. He pitched forward across the boardwalk, writhing.

After the report of the gun, the shocked silence was absolute, except for the panting breaths of the dying man until he, too, finally became silent, lay still.

Old Cal turned involuntarily to his companion, then remained motionless, watching the youth. Caspar's nostrils flared, his eyes blazed; he was breathing hard.

The sheriff came past them both and turned the body over with his foot. He shook his head slowly from side to side, then faced the now-muttering crowd.

'He's dead,' he said. 'And his blood is

on the head of every one of you.'

'Caspar shouldn't have shot him!' somebody shouted. Josh himself thought the youth had acted a little precipitately; but he did not say so. He shouted, 'Caspar was protecting the law as well as himself. This man,' he prodded the body with his toe, 'probably picked on the boy because he figured him to be the weakest among us. But Caspar's got more guts than the rest of you put together.'

'We could rush you,' yelled Coney. 'You wouldn't stand a chance!'

'Neither would you,' chortled happy Cal. 'With two bullets in your fat belly, you'd get trampled to a pulp.'

'You might get us,' agreed the sheriff, 'but a good many of you wouldn't live to talk about it. Give up this foolishness. Go home. It'll soon be dawn an' I'm thinking none of us will be as brave and hearty then.'

He had held authority in this town for a long time. In their sober times these people respected him and listened to him. They were sobering up now in the chill night. He was beginning to shame them and he knew it. A man had been killed uselessly and the one who had killed him, this nervous crippled youth who stood aghast on the edge of the boardwalk, was little to blame. They were all to blame and they were beginning to realize it. Even Coney was silent now. His erstwhile barman's jeering remarks had stripped him of his dignity and his leadership.

The sheriff pressed home his advantage. 'Go home, you people. You know me — surely you know by now that you can trust me. Leave the law to the law. I'm ashamed of you all. You, Jack . . . you, Sam . . . you, Isiah . . . ' He stabbed his finger at faces in the crowd in the half-light, and those faces were turned away. Maybe Josh was a little wasted as a tough Western lawman: maybe, with a little more education, he could have been a sweet-tongued Eastern senator.

The crowd swelled slowly, then began

to break away in little groups. Tired men, a little disgruntled and shame-faced, wended their way homewards to the arms, or the fists, of their waiting wives. Many of the single men were soon snapped up by percentage girls hovering near and led away to the quiet cribs on the edge of town.

The body of the shot man was dragged into the sheriff's office for the time being. Young Caspar was silent but unashamed as he accompanied Happy Cal to the lodging-house where they both stayed.

'I'm afraid this was my fault, Josh,' said Jay Simmonds. 'I'm a no-good, big-mouthed drunk.'

'Forget it, son,' said Josh, who knew how much it must have cost his arrogant deputy to make that abject apology. 'Let me take a look at that head o' yourn. What happened to it?'

'Somebody kicked some sense into it!'

* * *

As Tom Brenner ran away from the three men, he knew his limp must have given him away. Without his gun he felt helpless and savage. Any moment he expected to hear shots, to feel hot slugs biting into his body.

Surprise had halted the three men and given the fugitive a start. But now, after a flurry of indecision, they were in full cry after him. He turned into another alley, saw a door. He was surprised when he found it unlocked. He opened it, passed through into stygian darkness, closed it gently behind him. He breathed a sigh of relief when he heard the heavy boots thudding away.

He whirled at a sound, slapping his thigh where his gun should have been. He felt a moment of helpless panic as sudden yellow light half-blinded him. Was this the way he must finish, without even seeing the one who dealt the death-blow?

He felt overwhelming relief as a voice said softly, 'Take it easy, son. You're quite safe here.' He had only heard that voice a few times before, but he recognized it. He had liked its owner.

His limbs seemed suddenly drained of life. He groped for a nearby chair and let himself fall into it. Then he looked up at Bern Cantell, the undertaker.

'They think I killed old Charlie Bennett and the one at the bank. They were set on a lynching. The sheriff gave me a chance to make a break.'

It was only then he seemed to notice the gun in Cantell's hand. Then he seemed to get his breath back, and he asked flatly, tonelessly, 'Are you going to turn me in?'

'I respect Josh Penrose's judgement,' said Cantell, in his velvety voice. 'If he thought it was fair to give you a chance, a chance is what you'll continue to get. I don't think anybody will look for you here.'

The hum of the mob came dimly from the street. Both the listening men stiffened at the sound of a shot. 'Stay here,' said Cantell. 'I'll see if I can find out what's going on. I'll douse the light to be on the safe side.'

'Right.'

The place was plunged into darkness, but not before the seated Brenner had discovered that he was in the undertaking parlour of the establishment. And now his only companions were two shrouded bodies. One was that of Charlie Bennett, he figured, but he could not think who the other might be.

Bootheels thudded once more outside. Brenner rose, pressed himself against the door which led into the alley. He listened. The owners of the boots seemed to be jittering around a lot and, in the distance, Brenner thought he heard a voice shouting.

It seemed like he stood there, tautly, for countless ages, wishing he had a gun or any kind of weapon. He could hardly see his hand when he held it in front of his face — and dead men did not carry weapons.

But finally the footsteps faded away; there seemed to be a lull in the noise altogether.

Brenner might have smiled sardonically could he have followed his erstwhile pursuers and listened in on their conversation.

'You must've been seein' things, Hep,' said a burly young man.

'Go on, blame me!' retorted the diminutive Hep. 'You ran pretty fast after nuthin' anyway.'

'The ground must've opened up an' swallowed him,' said the third, a lanky beanpole. 'Either that or Coney's rotgut is making us all see things.'

'I'm sure he limped . . . '

'Well, how could he have gotten out . . . ?'

'Anyway, where could he have gone . . . ?'

'Everything seems kinda crazy. As for me, I'm all through playing tag. Let's go an' see what that shooting was all about.' The burly young man led the way.

'It's getting mighty quiet out there,' said the beanpole as they turned into the alley alongside the jail.

'Looks like they're breakin' up,' said little Hep, as they got closer.

The burly young man broke away from the alley first and almost ran into a percentage girl, a comely half-caste. She linked her arm with his and smiled up at him, her dark eyes inviting.

'What's happened, honey?' he asked.

'The party's over, *chiquita*. Everybody wishes to go to bed.'

'Best place for 'em.'

He put his arm around the girl's waist and they moved away together.

'That's the right idea, I guess,' said the beanpole. He sighed. 'Hell, I wish my missus wasn't so goshdarned fat.'

'Women!' said little Hep, and spat. 'Me I'm gonna angle a bottle of rye from Coney's before he closes the bar. That's all the comfort I need for this night.'

*   *   *

Jay Simmonds' mood of humble co-operation was shattered a little when he learned that his boss had let their prize jailbird escape.

'He probably got clean away, too,' he grumbled. 'We ain't heard any alarm.'

'If he has it can't be helped,' said Josh quietly, a little wearily. 'All we had against him was a tissue of circumstantial evidence. Somehow, I don't think he'll run far.'

'You think he has some reason for wantin' to come back to Lagos?'

'That could be,' said Josh.

But Jay, for once, did not seem inclined to debate about it. His wounded temple, beneath the cocoon of bandages with which Josh had festooned it, throbbed alarmingly. 'I think I better go home to bed.'

'Sure, Jay. Will you be all right?'

'Yeh, I'll be all right, thanks. What about Jimmy here?' Jimmy had been a drunkard who also claimed to be a prospector and came into Lagos from time to time seeking excitement. He had been a born troublemaker, and folks had said he must get his dinero other ways than in prospecting, he wasn't the type to work. Jimmy hadn't been very popular and was no big loss to the community: he had never really been a member of it anyway.

'We'll let Bern Cantell have him in the mornin',' said Josh. He crossed to his desk and produced a flat bottle half-full of liquor. He handed it to Jay. 'Hair of the cur that bit you. Take it home with you — have a snort before retiring. It'll kill the pain in your head an' help you to sleep.'

Jay smiled crookedly. 'Thanks, Josh. All things considered, you're bein' mighty good to me.'

Josh grinned beneath his walrus moustache. 'Forget it. I've often felt like kickin' you in the head myself. Mebbe now I'm just bein' apologetic. You go home to bed now. An' I should let Doc Limpole take a look at that head before you come to work in the morning.'

'Right, Josh. Goodnight.'

'An' Jay . . . '

'Yeh?'

'Keep your mouth shut about Tom Brenner's escape.'

Simmonds grinned ruefully. 'Seems like it ain't lucky for me to open my mouth. I'll keep it shut this time all right old-timer. You can depend on me.'

'I hope so,' said Josh Penrose softly, as the door closed behind his deputy.

He locked and bolted the door, then climbed the stairs to his bedroom above the jail. His emotions about tonight's furore were a little mixed. He could have died tonight, violently. But that had happened before, so he did not think about it. He was not quite so proud of his own part in tonight's affair as he might have been. He need not have been so eager to let Tom Brenner free. That might cause complications later.

Nevertheless, on reflection, he decided he probably had not seen the last of that limping, grim-looking younker.

8

Tom Brenner blinked as the yellow light flashed on again. His eyes focused on Bern Cantell. Then he saw that there was somebody else coming out of the shadows in the passage behind the undertaker. For a moment he had the feeling he had been betrayed, but that was before he realized that the newcomer was a girl, and then he was surprised, a little ashamed, a little confused.

She was a lovely girl, too, as she stood looking at him, straining her dark eyes against the yellow light. Hair black as a raven's wing, tied in tight coils round her head for sleeping; small trim figure seductively rounded in the belted dressing-gown.

'This is my daughter, Louise,' said Bern Cantell. 'She, naturally, wanted to know what the noise was about.'

'She can at least take a look at the reason for the noise,' said Tom Brenner.

He bowed slightly. The girl returned his oblique greeting with a grave inclination of her head. Her father had not mentioned Brenner's name. Brenner himself figured the undertaker must have already told his daughter of the identity of the nocturnal visitor. A suspected murderer, hunted like an animal. But there was no censure in her gaze, only a polite friendliness.

She said. 'Things have quietened down now. I think I will go back to bed. Goodnight.'

Both men said goodnight. Then Cantell closed the door behind her and came further into the room, to Brenner. He told him of what, as far as he had been able to make out, had transpired.

'A man was killed,' he concluded. 'I don't know who, but I know it wasn't one of those on the side of the law. I'll soon find out in the morning, I guess,' he added, with dry humour.

'I'm mighty obliged to you, Mr

Cantell,' said Brenner. 'I'll be on my way before I cause you any real trouble.'

'There'll be no more trouble for a while. Folks have cooled down. They'll begin to reason with themselves, realize they were led into things by drink and a few hotheaded characters. Were you aiming to leave Lagos altogether?'

'And make everybody believe I'm really guilty? No!' Brenner shook his head from side to side. 'I'll just lay low outside for a while then come back. Nobody will know I've ever been in your place.'

His voice carried conviction. But there was no evidence in Cantell's smooth, kindly face as to whether he believed Brenner or not. The undertaker said, 'I'm not worried about whether people know you've been here or not. I've handled the people of Lagos, living and dead, since the place was just a dried waterhole. They do not trouble me.' There was humour, but no hint of boastfulness. Cantell went on:

'You would be welcome to stay here and rest. Nobody will find you here — it is not the kind of place people visit voluntarily. But everything comes to me eventually, in more ways than one, and you will be able to learn what is going on far more easily than you would in some hidey-hole outside.'

Maybe it was a test, or even a trap. Brenner's face was expressionless, but it was evident he was pondering. Cantell went on, almost persuasively. 'We have an attic with a spare bed we keep for visitors. It is reached by the back stairs there. Nobody could interfere with you.'

He pointed to the corner of the undertaking parlour to where narrow wooden stairs, little more than a ladder, angled upwards to a balcony which the light did not quite reach. Shadows lurked. Cantell said, 'This part of the establishment used to be stables before they were converted. Up there used to be a loft.'

'You're takin' a big chance,' said

Brenner bluntly. 'Havin' a killer to lodge with you.'

Cantell did not contradict him; merely said, 'Let me be the judge of that. Stay the rest of the night anyway.'

Was this the test? Brenner weighed it, made his decision. 'Thank you, Mr Cantell,' he said, and turned towards the stairs.

'We are both tired, no doubt,' said the undertaker. 'We will talk further in the morning. But do not show yourself until I call you. I daresay I shall have customers in the morning, one of whom, at least, will be semi-permanent. Goodnight.'

'Goodnight.'

'Have you matches? Mr Brenner?'

'Yes.'

'If you can manage then I will turn out the light. It might draw attention. You will find a lamp in the attic.'

'Thank you.'

The light went out. Brenner had reached the balcony. Now he groped in the pitch darkness for lucifers and found them. He struck one and held it aloft. Straightaway he saw the door in the long wall at the back of the balcony. As he opened it, his match went out and he stumbled into more steps he had not expected. Another light proved to him that they were only a short flight. He climbed them and ducked through the doorless aperture at the top and found himself, at last, in the attic.

The first thing he assured himself of was that there were heavy curtains at the tiny window. He opened the window, taking deep breaths of the cool night air before closing the curtains tightly. The place smelled musty, unused. He found the lamp on the tiny table. Everything had a thick layer of dust. There were a couple of chairs, too, and an ancient chest of drawers. As well as the truckle bed laid with rough blankets. And everything thick with dust, except the blankets when he shook them: they seemed pretty fresh and the undersheet was, of course, white and fresh.

His head almost touching the bare rafters, Brenner stood in the middle of the tiny room and looked about him. The flickering lamplight threw his grotesque shadow on the walls and ceiling. He did not like that hole there, leading on to the second flight of steps. No door to shut, no protection: a man could poke his head and shoulders through there and, without leaving the steps, could fill anybody in the room with gun-slugs. No cover.

Brenner got hold of the chest of drawers and dragged them half across the gap, so that they shielded the bed. The drawers felt light, empty, but he did not bother to investigate them. He yawned, stretched, sat on the edge of the bed to take off his boots. He did not have a gunbelt to take off and, for a moment, was a little nonplussed. A man might need a gun under his pillow in a strange place like this. He climbed into bed just as he was. The sheets closed gently over him and for a moment he thought irritationally, but quite naturally, of the dark girl sleeping in another part of the building. And so, he slept, too.

He awoke to find daylight filtering through the curtains. From down below came the rumble of voices. He was instantly alert. He got from the bed and padded across the room in stockinged feet. He discovered then that he could squeeze past the chest of drawers without moving them. He descended the first flight of steps and opened the door gently.

After a little manoeuvring, finally standing on tiptoe on the bottom step, he could see across the balcony and down to the floor of the undertaking parlour. His lips tightened at what he saw.

There were four men there. Sheriff Penrose, Jay Simmonds, Bern Cantell and Bern's gangling assistant, Mack. Perhaps it would've been more correct to figure five men. Though the fifth was laid out on trestles and the other four were gazing down on him. This was, no doubt, the *hombre* who had gotten himself killed last night.

The rumble of voices was much louder now, but, although Brenner strained his ears, he could not catch any words. Jay Simmonds was hatless and his head was swathed in white bandages. Brenner wondered who had laced the fancy-pants deputy.

Brenner stiffened as the little group broke apart. Had Cantell sold him out? But the men only crossed to another trestle and Cantell lifted the brown sheet a little so that they could look at the face. Whose face? Charlie Bennett's? Although Brenner craned his neck he could not see.

Mack had thrown a sheet over the body of the new arrival and now Cantell had covered the other face up, too, and the company was moving towards the door. The sheriff turned to deliver some parting remark, then he and his deputy passed out of sight.

Cantell sent his assistant out on some errand. Then he came to the bottom of the stairs and called, 'Brenner.' The young man stepped out on to the balcony, made for the stairs.

'The sheriff will be back soon,' said Cantell urgently.

Brenner halted at the top step. 'What's goin' on?'

'We just brought in the man who got killed last night. He isn't much loss to anybody as far as I know. But the sheriff wants folks in town to take a look — in a sort of identification parade — at the man they found dead out on the desert yesterday.'

Brenner, still in his stockinged feet, began to descend the stairs. His limp was very noticeable. 'You mean the dead man they mentioned when they met the posse on the trail last night?'

'Yes.'

'The existence of that other body had slipped my memory,' said Brenner. 'Let me take a look at him.'

'You think you might know him?' It could have been a question. Or a statement. Brenner didn't say anything, but passed the undertaker.

Instinct seemed to lead him to the right trestle. He uncovered the face.

'Hurry up, Brenner,' said Cantell. 'The sheriff will be back soon.'

The young man drew the sheet back into position, turned away from the body 'I never saw that man before,' he pronounced.

'The lawmen think he might be one of the hold-up men. Anyway, they are going to get as many townsfolk as they can to look at this corpse in the hopes that somebody might identify the man . . .'

Cantell broke off, flapped his hands, an unusual sign of agitation for him. 'Get back upstairs. I'll see if I can smuggle some breakfast up to you before anybody else gets here.'

'That's mighty kind of you.'

Brenner climbed the stairs once more and vanished into the gloom above.

Some minutes later he began to tiptoe across the floor of his den as he heard the door open below. From the cavity behind the chest of drawers a voice issued.

'Can I come up, Mr Brenner?'

He relaxed; a sweet female voice, too.

'Certainly,' he called.

As he pushed the chest of drawers to one side the girl's head came through the aperture. She had let her hair down and it flowed in glossy raven coils to her shoulders. Her dark eyes looked up into his, her soft red lips parted. Brenner felt the warm blood coursing beneath the skin of his face. Not until she said, a little sharply, 'Will you take this from me, Mr Brenner?' did he realize she was holding a tray.

He realized he had been staring, too. He took the tray hastily. 'Thank you, miss. Thank you very much.'

'Father says I must go right down,' she said. 'I will pick up the tray later.'

Her head disappeared and he was left half-bending, a little stupidly, holding the tray. Only then did he become cognizant of its contents and of the delectable smell arising from it, too.

Two eggs, fried sunny-side up; crisp rashers; buckwheat cakes and syrup; a pot of coffee; a packet of store cigarettes. The Cantells were certainly doing their tame killer proud. He carried the food over to the bed, drew up a chair, and set to.

He left the food when he heard movements downstairs. Through the slightly opened bottom door he saw some of the townsfolk, shepherded by Sheriff Penrose, begin to file into the undertaking parlour. Doubtless, Deputy Simmonds was still out rounding up others. Brenner could not hear what was being said, so he returned to his food before it got cold.

*　　*　　*

The atmosphere of the undertaking parlour had a subtle effect on the visiting townsmen. The benches, the dark curtains, the scrubbed floor and smell of carbolic, the empty trestles waiting, the two shrouded forms

. . . and above all, the third form with the bleak face uncovered, the eyes staring upwards. They filed past that staring face. They gave it short glances and shook their heads, passing on, glad to escape to the warmth and the sunshine outside once more.

Sheriff Penrose watched them come and go, his own face expressionless, his mouth drooping a little beneath his walrus moustache. This was rather an unorthodox procedure and Josh knew by the townsfolks' manner that they were acutely aware of it. Nobody had seen the dead stranger before, it seemed. Maybe he hadn't been one of the bank-robbers after all. Anyway, very few folks had seen the robbers, maybe nobody had really had a good look at them. Poor Billy's two colleagues, the assistant bank manager and another teller had already seen the dead man. They could not commit themselves because they had only seen the backs of the robbers.

Jay Simmonds entered with more townspeople, among them Happy Cal and his young pardner, Caspar. Of these two, Cal reached the trestle first. He looked down on its burden and cackled.

'He looks just like my nephew, George. 'Cept George has only one ear — a Cherokee Injun got the other one, funniest thing you . . . '

'All right, Cal,' interrupted Jay Simmonds. 'You're holdin' up the squad.'

The atmosphere of the undertaking parlour or the presence of the law didn't seem to throw a crimp in Cal's tail. Still chortling, he passed on and young Caspar lurched into his place.

The younker looked fixedly at the dead face. His own face was almost as ashen. 'Take the sheet off an' let's see the rest of him,' he said hoarsely.

Jay Simmonds laughed hoarsely. 'Why, kid?'

'Do as he says,' said Sheriff Penrose sharply.

Simmonds did as he was told, removing the brown sheet with a contemptuous flick of his wrist. Caspar limped a little nearer, rested his hand on the edge of the trestle to steady himself. He took a good look at the body in its worn and dusty clothes.

'Did he have a hat?'

'No, we didn't find a hat,' said the sheriff.

'I would've liked to see him in a hat.'

'Try mine,' said old Cal. 'I ain't partickler. Maybe the cuss 'ull bring me luck.'

Jay Simmonds took the battered slouch and placed it on the dead man's head.

'I'm pretty sure he was one o' the bank-robbers,' said young Caspar.

Everybody stirred a little, made noises. But nobody spoke until the sheriff said, 'We didn't know you saw the robbers, Caspar.'

'I'd just been in the feed-barn. I came face to face with them as they left the bank. If I hadn't dodged back into the barn they might've plugged me.'

'Why didn't you tell us before?'

'Nobody asked me,' retorted Caspar defiantly. 'Nobody ever asks me anything.' Two spots of colour burned on his pallid checks.

'All right, son,' said Josh Penrose gently. 'Don't get your dander up.'

Caspar was a little mollified. 'Of course, I can't be sure about this,' he said, jerking a thumb in the direction of the corpse. 'Both men were masked. But he certainly looks like the one who was nearest to me.'

'How about the other one,' asked Josh softly, 'what was he like?'

'I didn't see him so well.'

'Stay a mite, Caspar,' said the sheriff, and swung away from the youth. He raised his voice. 'That's all for a while, folks.'

Jay Simmonds exchanged glances with his superior, raised his eyebrows a little, but began to shepherd the rest of the townspeople through the door leading into the alley.

'Would you like me to leave for a while, too, sheriff?' purred Bern Cantell.

'Yes, Bern — if you wouldn't mind.'

'No. Not at all.' Jay Simmonds closed the door behind Cantell then turned to the sheriff and Caspar standing alone in the centre of the floor.

Josh drew the sheet up over the body. 'Now, Caspar,' he said. 'See if you can describe the other man.'

'I don't think I can — really.'

Josh said softly, 'Think hard. Did he look anything like the man we know as Tom Brenner?'

'No, I don't think he did,' said Caspar instantly. 'The man was shorter and tubbier.'

'An' yet a minute or two ago you said you didn't get a good look at this second geezer,' put in Jay Simmonds harshly.

Caspar turned on the deputy like a twisted animal. 'Don't crowd me,' he said hoarsely. 'I meant I didn't see his face . . . *I didn't see his face.*'

'You couldn't have seen his face, anyway, if he wore a mask.'

'The other one wore a mask, too, but it only covered his nose and chin. I saw the rest of his face pretty plainly, that's why I think this is the man.' Caspar made a violent gesture towards the corpse.

'All right, son,' said Josh Penrose. 'You can go.'

Without another word, Caspar left the place.

Jay Simmonds said, a little defiantly, 'Do you think I rode him too hard?'

'No, I don't think so. Caspar told all he could, I guess — or all he aimed to tell. I guess we can take it pretty much for granted that this dead man was one of the bank robbers. The black kerchief; Caspar's testimony — it all ties up.'

'Yeh,' said Simmonds. Then he went off at a tangent. 'Caspar seemed too eager to defend Tom Brenner. They've been hobnobbing in Coney's place. Brenner has a way with him. Mebbe

Caspar's begun to hero-worship him or somethin'.'

'It was more than hero-worship that made Caspar face that mob in front of the jail last night,' said the sheriff. 'The boy's got guts.'

There was a knock on the door and the sheriff called, 'Come in.' Bern Cantell popped his head round the corner. 'Have you finished, gentlemen? I have to prepare poor Charlie for the funeral this afternoon.'

'We'll be at the funeral,' said Jay Simmonds hastily. 'But the preparation you can handle alone.' He preceded his superior from the undertaking parlour.

9

The sun blazed down on the dry cart-rutted main street of Lagos. Blazed down on the silent watchers along one boardwalk, threw sombre shadows over those on the other side. Blazed down on the people who walked in the centre of the street, for they had no cover at all. Blazed down on the pine coffin borne by four of Charlie Bennett's best friends.

Charlie had loved the sun, it would not have caused him any discomfort. The sun; the breeze from the desert, blowing fitfully, raising little puffs of dust beneath the slowly-pacing feet.

It was a real old-time Western funeral. There was not a horse in sight. Main Street had been cleared. Folks unused to walking walked now, many of them in high-heeled riding-boots because they were the only kind of boots they owned. But even this sweating, arch-crippling torture was welcome, their tribute to old Charlie, whom everybody had loved.

Main Street opened out; and there was the slope leading up to Boot Hill. The coffin tilted perilously as its bearers bent at the knees, toiling sweatily upwards. Josh Penrose, representing the law, Doc Limpole, Lagos's only medico, who had treated Charlie for many bumps, scratches and doses of fever, as well as played checkers with him many times into the small hours. Bern Cantell, like Charlie, one of nature's gentlemen, too; with loving care he had prepared his old friend for his last timeless journey. Lemmy Dricourt, Charlie's old drinking partner, for once sober, his huge figure bowed not with the weight of the casket, but with silent grief. The old ones. The young ones could sneer at them, but the old ones, like Charlie, were part of a West that would soon be fading. Hard-talking, hard-fighting, hard-drinking men, but staunch to their particular code; nature's gentlemen.

Boot Hill was reached and, from behind the glade of trees on the summit, the preacher walked. Sep Lorimer, affectionately known as 'The Groaner.' His plump figure was faultlessly attired in black broad-cloth. He scorned the Eastern method of wearing a stiff collar back to front. His collar was of soft white silk, decorated by a stylishly-knotted black string tie. His weatherbeaten face was set in its usual lugubrious expression and his brown spaniel eyes were downcast. Sep was proud of his clothes and his craft; he was somewhat of a showman, but a good man to boot. Charlie Bennett had also been his friend.

The town would pay him well for this particular funeral. Money to buy more clothes for the glory of the Lord; just a little to keep body and soul together; the rest (he always made sure that there would be a little left over) would go to fatherless children or other cases which were deserving of his charity.

The wind up here on Boot Hill was clean and keen, sweeping the landscape bare of the dust that irritated the town, bringing the scent of desert vegetation, rustling the brown grass with a gentle whispering sound. Old Charlie would rest well here, overlooking the town where he had drunk and dreamed, given pleasure and raised hell.

As the coffin was lowered into the ground, Sep Lorimer began his groaning oration. He sounded like an overgrown bullfrog in tears. But there was no room for laughter now in the hearts of his hearers. The words were good and it was the words they heard: a last tribute to Charlie from an old friend, from many old friends . . .

'The Groaner' had finished his oration and dirt was trickling on to the coffin-lid as folks filed past to pay their last tribute to Charlie Bennett, when the horesman came riding up the hill, shouting, and the scene changed rapidly.

Those at the back heard the rider's words first. They scattered in all directions away from him. Some of them ran down the hill towards the town. The horseman rode through, onwards. People scattered from the graveside. The horseman reined in at the edge of the grave, his horse snorting pawing the earth. More earth reined in on the coffin. The grave-diggers raised their shovels like weapons.

The rider was a hostler who worked at one of the stables down below. He was hatless. His face was red and perspiring and he gasped for breath.

One of the men grabbed the horse's reins and pulled him away from the edge of the grave. 'What's the meaning of this?' said 'The Groaner' in terrible tones. But the hostler had shouted his voice away and, for a moment, could only gulp like a fish.

Sheriff Penrose, Lemmy Dricourt, Bern Cantell, Doc Limpole, they all gathered around the simpleton of a rider. Jay Simmonds came running up, a gun in his hand. 'Speak up, man,' boomed Herculean Lemmy, jabbing at the horseman's thigh with a blunt forefinger.

But it was the sight of the gun in Jay Simmonds' hand which finally released the flood of words.

'Somebody stuck up the bank . . . stuck up the bank. Mackey got shot . . . ' Mackey was the hostler's employee. Jay Simmonds whirled, ran down the slope. The others streamed after him. The two grave diggers lowered their shovels.

'Finish your job,' said Sep Lorimer harshly.

A little sheepishly the two men bent once more to their task. Out of the corner of his mouth, one said to the other, 'Wherever he his, I'll bet old Charlie is laughin' his goshdarned head off.'

Main Street was in an uproar. Doc Limpole ran into the stables to see Mackey, who, luckily, had only a slug in his shoulder. The way of the sheriff and the rest was blocked by clamouring townsfolk. Questions flew thick and fast. Seemed like nobody knew any answers. The little fat bank manager teetered on the steps of the bank and yelled himself purple in the face. He had been out of town when the last bank job had been pulled. He had been bragging ever since that the robbers had got away with next to nothing . . . next to nothing . . . Of course, there was young Billy . . . but these things happened . . .

According to the tubby manager's demeanour, the robber or robbers had gotten away with a little more than 'next to nothing' this time. And doubtless a few sardonic folks got a kind of depraved satisfaction in watching the little man dance upon his steps.

The sheriff forced his way through. The bank manager grabbed the lawman by the lapels of the black store-suit he had donned specially for the funeral. The little fat man babbled words into the sheriff's face.

Another masked man . . . just one was all he had seen . . . only three men in the bank . . . hadn't a chance; had to hand over a lot of money.

The two employees joined their boss. They could not say more than the fat man's incoherent ramblings had already told the sheriff. The bandit had been heavily masked. They had not had a good look at him. Maybe, remembering what had happened to young Billy on the previous occasion, they had been too scared to do anything but exactly what the bandit told them. Maybe they had not dared to look at him too closely.

He had made them hand over all the loose money. He had made the manager open the little safe — the one where more loose cash was kept — and empty that. He had dropped everything into a gunny-sack. Then he had told them all to turn their backs — if they moved he would shoot. None of them had turned till they heard the shot from outside, the drum of hooves . . .

Sheriff Penrose, followed by Jay and Lemmy, forced himself through the crowd once more to the stables. Nobody seemed to notice Bern Cantell detach himself from the group and make his way back to the undertaking parlour. Mackey, the wounded stableman, was sitting up on a couch in his living-quarters with his arm in a sling.

'He'll be all right,' said Doc Limpole. Sheriff Penrose asked, 'Feel like talking?'

'I'll say I do,' exploded Mackey. 'That gink must've known the town was half-empty. He left his horse in the alley side o' my place as calm as you please. He must've led the horse up the alley, 'cos I didn't see him pass my front. The thick dust drifts into the alley and would muffle the hoofbeats. I didn't see the man until he was mounting the horse. I saw him sling his bag across the saddle. He still had his mask on. I grabbed my shotgun and stepped outside. He spotted me before I had chance to call him. What with the bag

126

an' everythin', I didn't realize he still had his gun in his hand till he fired. Next thing I knew, I was lying on my back on the boardwalk, chewing his dust as he went past, an' feelin' as if a mule had kicked me.'

'What did he look like?' asked Josh.

'About medium height, I guess. Lean. I didn't get a real good look at him.'

'Did you see him walkin'?'

'He was gettin' on his horse when I spotted him.'

'Did he limp?' put in Jay Simmonds.

'I told you,' snorted Mackey. 'He was gettin' on his horse.'

Josh turned towards his deputy; said sardonically, 'You forgot to ask the folks in the bank that question, Jay.'

'So did you,' retorted Simmonds hotly.

'I wouldn't have seen him at all if I hadn't had a sick horse on my hands,' said Mackey. 'I'd've been up on the hill paying my last respects to ol' Charlie if this horse hadn't took sick . . .'

'Where was Luke when you got shot?' put in Josh Penrose. Luke was the dim-witted hostler who had given the alarm.

Mackey said, 'I'd sent him down the street to get some tar. He came back an' picked me up. But he hadn't seen hide or hair o' the one who did the shooting.'

'Nobody saw nothin',' burst out Jay Simmonds. He turned violently on his heels. 'I'm going back to the bank,' he called over his shoulder.

* * *

Louise Cantell met her father at the door of their place. 'What's going on?'

'Somebody robbed the bank.' Bern was unusually agitated. 'Where's Tom Brenner?'

'I dunno. Still upstairs, I guess. He was up there when I fetched the tray back.'

'How long was that ago?'

'Huh, about an hour, I guess. Father, you don't think . . . '

128

She broke off; he was already making his way through the place. She flung a last glance back at the crowds in the street then she followed him. And, as she followed him, she began to get scared.

He stopped in the undertaking parlour and took a gun from the cupboard in the wall. This gave her a chance to catch him up. She was right behind him as he climbed the stairs to the loft. They reached the balcony.

'Stay here, girl,' he said.

'But, father . . . '

'Do as I say!'

She nodded mutely. He opened the door, ascended the smaller flight of stairs, passed out of her sight.

His footsteps faded. There was no sound. She put her clenched fist to her mouth and bit the knuckles. Her eyes widened with tension, with pain.

Finally she could contain herself no longer. She started forward, flung the door wide so that it crashed against the wall behind. She barked her knees as she went up the wooden steps at an alarming rate. She disregarded the pain.

When her father's face looked, surprisedly, down at her, she felt faint with relief. He had to grab her hand and pull her up beside him.

'He's gone,' he said flatly.

She looked a little dazedly around the small bare room. The bed was neatly made; it was as if there had never been anybody there.

'What was he doing when you fetched the tray?'

'Standing smoking, peering through the window.'

'Did he say anything to you, do anything?'

The girl coloured slightly. 'He didn't say, or do, anything strange, if that's what you mean.'

'I trusted him,' said Bern, half to himself. 'I left him here alone with you. I left the place open. Wide open. I thought I could judge him. Maybe I'm spending so much time with dead people I'm beginning to lose my touch with the living.'

10

She had heard him pad across the tiny room. His shadow had fallen across the tray, then it had moved and when she put her head through the aperture he was standing by the window, blue smoke spiralling upwards from the cigarette in his mouth.

He turned slowly and she felt once more the impact of his strange eyes. But they became friendly as well as enquiring as he looked at her and she heard herself say, a little inanely, 'I've come for the tray.'

She saw how bad his limp was as he crossed to the bed, then she realized that he was still in his stockinged feet and that would make his lopsided walk seem worse. If she felt a spasm of pity, she tried not to show it, for, despite his limp, he was a comely young man. Lithe, strong, strangely attractive. She beat him to the bed and felt herself colouring as she lifted the tray. She remained stooped a little longer than was necessary and the scarlet flood subsided as quickly as it had come.

She was glad he did not look at her directly as he said, 'You are very good to me, miss. I suppose you know why I'm here.'

'I know.'

She knew what he was getting at and lowered her head, a little frightened of what she might see in those bold, eloquent eyes of his. She suddenly realized what a chance her father might be taking in having this man here. What a risk she might be taking, too — being here.

But she was not scared of him. More scared of herself and her sudden schoolgirlish tremors. There was a strong elemental power about this young man: it seemed to radiate from him. She thought he must be attractive to women. She didn't know whether she was attracted by him. Maybe she was even repelled a little. She had heard of killer's eyes. Those eyes of his: were they killer's eyes? They certainly had a strange effect on her!

She suddenly realized she was thinking like a schoolgirl now as well as acting like one, standing there gawkily, silently. Seemed like *he* could remain silent as long as *she* chose, without being at all ill at ease. Or, even if he was ill at ease, he disguised the fact pretty well. That lean, dark killer's face: was that a poker-face, too . . . ? She turned almost violently away from him and made for the trap.

The tray tilted and a plate and fork clattered to the floor. She bent and, as she did so, Brenner went past her. Their heads knocked gently. She looked into his face and though her own was scarlet, she was glad to see that, at last, he was showing a little discomfiture, too. He had hold of the plate and fork and as she straightened up, he straightened up with her and placed the utensils on the tray. Then he smiled and, despite herself, she began to smile, too, and, next moment, they were both laughing openly.

He laughed like somebody who was unused to laughing. Not raucously and artificially like your life-of-the-party sort of fellow, but deeply, vibrantly, his head thrown back and his body shaking. The sight of him laughing like that with such huge enjoyment as if something had been set free inside him only made her worse, and she lost her balance and fell helplessly against him.

His arm went round her and he held her and they both stopped laughing as suddenly as they had begun. He could not hold her close because the tray was in the way, its rim digging into his stomach. She used the tray as a sort of lever to straighten herself up and his arm slid away from her. She was frightened of what might happen next, so she turned away, went through the trap.

He called after her vibrantly. 'Can I help?'

'No, thank you. I can manage. Father said you ought to stay there.'

They were back on the old footing. The hunted killer; the charitable daughter. But a little something still remained from the in-between time, a little something which brought a flush to the girl's cheeks as she crossed the silent undertaking parlour.

★　★　★

Bern Cantell stood with the gun in his hand and looked around the room. His daughter watched him half-fearfully. Neither of them spoke. Bern spun on his heels suddenly and went across to the small window and looked out. Nothing out there seemed to reassure him. He turned again.

'I'm an old fool,' he said. 'An old fool . . . What do you think, girl?'

'I don't think you're an old fool, father.'

'That isn't what I'm asking you. You know what I mean.'

She hesitated and her face was a little flushed. At last she said, 'I'm like you, I guess. I don't know what to think.'

Bern looked at his daughter strangely. Then he said flatly, as if he had come to a decision: 'I know what I think.'

He strode past her and descended the stairs. She followed more slowly, a bewildered look on her face. When she got down to the undertaking parlour her father was over at the cupboard in the corner, the cupboard where he kept two spare guns. It was usually locked, but now, for some reason, or just through somebody's carelessness, it was unlocked. Louise remembered how her father had snatched one gun from there as he passed through on his way upstairs. She was sure he had not had time to unlock it. Had the door, perhaps, been forced? It looked all right . . . Then she saw her father take the second gun out of the cupboard; and then he turned towards her, holding a weapon in each hand.

He turned away from her again and,

still carrying the guns, went through into the living-quarters. He kept another gun in the kitchen drawer. That proved to be still there, too.

When Bern spoke, it was as if he was talking to himself. 'I'll have to tell Josh Penrose. A man doesn't like to admit he's been a fool, and a criminal fool at that — but the law has got to be told.'

'Perhaps he'll come back,' said Louise.

'Brenner?'

'Yes.'

'Do you think he will?'

'I-I don't know.'

'Why should he come back?' asked Bern.

He did not wait for an answer. From the window, Louise watched him wending his way through the crowd towards the bank.

★ ★ ★

Sheriff Penrose had followed his deputy to the bank. Jay was already interrogating the bank manager and his two assistants. All four of them were by now

137

a little red in the face.

Jay turned on his superior officer. 'The bandit limped.'

'I . . . ' began the little manager, and spluttered into silence.

'Who says he did?'

'They say so. This one!'

The young bank cashier indicated backed away a little from Simmonds' stabbing forefinger.

'I couldn't be sure. I thought maybe. I . . . '

'You said he limped,' said Simmonds savagely, and started forward, his hands rising as if he would clutch the man by the throat.

Josh grabbed his arm. 'Hold it! If he said the man limped, mebbe you stuck the words into his mouth.'

Now Simmonds rounded on his boss.

'You're makin' excuses for that *hombre* all the time! Are you just blind — or is there some other reason?'

Josh let go of the younger man's wrist. 'Don't be a fool.' He was perfectly cool, but there was an edge to his voice.

The lean old-timer and the big florid young man stood eyeing each other, symbols of the ageless battle. And it was at this juncture that Bern Cantell entered the bank.

'I must see you, Josh,' he said, and took the sheriff urgently aside.

Instinctively, because he was the law, too, Jay Simmonds followed. He heard the undertaker's hurried story and when it was finished, he said:

'What did I tell yuh? Ain't that conclusive?'

Josh Penrose ignored his deputy. To Cantell he said, 'I guess I can't blame you, Bern. I gave the younker his first break. I'm as much to blame as you are.'

'An' while you stand gabbing, he's gettin' further an' further away,' said Jay Simmonds.

He whirled on his heels and made for the door.

'Wait a minute, Jay,' said the sheriff.

But the door was already swinging behind the deputy and, if he had heard his superior's call, he chose not to heed it. Townsfolk yelled questions at him as he forced his way through the crowd. His eyes looked savagely ahead, he heeded nobody. He went to the stables and got his horse and, using the back way to avoid the mob, rode out of town. He had gathered from Mackey which direction the bank-robber had taken. The skunk was probably making for the hills. Simmonds fixed his eyes on their shimmering outlines and spurred his mount to greater speed.

When Josh Penrose got out on to the steps of the bank, he could not see his deputy anywhere. But it did not strain his grey matter none to figure out where the young fool had gone. Questions were thrown at him. He raised his hands. 'Hold your horses,' he shouted.

The clamour died. He went on: 'I want a posse. Ten men will do.'

About three dozen yelling volunteers pushed their way forward. Bern Cantell said into the sheriff's ear, 'Count me in.'

'One,' said Josh, grimly humorous.

He picked Lemmy Dricourt, too. Doc Limpole said regretfully he'd have to stay in town in case he got some more patients. Happy Cal got to go, and so did his pardner, Caspar. After the cripple youth's showing in front of the mob the day before, Josh had not the heart to turn him down. Maybe the boy would be useful — if he didn't get too trigger-happy. Coney had gotten another relief-barman from someplace, so the fat man came. He was quite a subdued fat man now: Josh figured he wouldn't get any more lynch-talk from the saloon-owner.

Josh carefully picked three more reliable men. They all got their horses and met at the edge of town, from where they were cheered on by the more enthusiastic of the populace, as well as a myriad of small boys.

⋆ ⋆ ⋆

The dying sun gave the buttes a blood-red tint. The shadows between them were of different graduations of violet. The sky touching the buttes was delicately rainbow-tinted. All the colours known to man were here at sundown in this wild, strange, lawless land. A painter would have raved about those colours — many painters had. But in the heart of the rider as he pushed his horse forward there was no place now for an appreciation of beauty.

He was perspiring, panting a little. His horse, lathered with sweat, began to slow down as if in protest at the pace which had been forced upon him over these countless miles. The rider gave the beast his own way now, but only because it suited him to do so. He was peering cautiously at the rocks in front as he drew near to them. He dropped one hand to his gun. A bushwacker could be lurking in those rocks, or up above with a rifle, waiting to pick him off.

There was a large outcrop of boulders between the rider and the foot of the hills. He steered his horse towards these rocks, urged him forward again. The beast responded and carried his master to safety.

Jay Simmonds dismounted. He took his canteen from the saddle and shook it. There was very little water left, and he had no food at all along with him. He was beginning to wish that he had not left Lagos in such an all-fired hurry.

He let himself fall against the rock and slid into a sitting position. He took off his hat and mopped his streaming face and sore forehead with his bandanna. Then the next moment he was on his feet again. He could not rest. He had not seen hide nor hair of man or beast during his long forced ride, but he might be nearing the end of his quest now.

He looked cautiously around the edge of the outcrop, searched the foothills in the failing light. A little breeze ruffled his hair. The wound in his skull itched abominably. After the heat the night atmosphere might become very cold and he had not brought a slicker or a blanket-coat. He drew his lips back from his teeth and slammed his hat once more on his head. He mounted his horse and rode away from the outcrop. He found the narrow pass and entered it.

The shadows were deepening, and when he came suddenly upon the other rider around a bend, he was almost taken by surprise, he had not heard a sound. The horse was broadside across the narrow trail as if the rider had urged it down the slope at the side, urged it from the peaks above. The rider was Tom Brenner and there was something slung across the saddle in front of him.

Jay Simmonds went for his gun. Tom Brenner pulled savagely at his horses' reins and the beast snorted and reared. Simmonds' horse was scared by this manoeuvre and backed rapidly, throwing the deputy off balance. Simmonds' gun went off in his hand — he was hardly aware that he had pulled the trigger. The slug ricocheted and whined in the rocks above. Simmonds came suddenly face to face with Brenner and his gun was knocked from his hand. He retaliated with clenched fist, feeling his knuckles smack against the other man's cheekbone. Brenner swayed, then came back again. His arms wrapped around Simmonds' waist. Locked together, the two men fell from their horses and rolled on the ground. Snorting with terror, both horses bolted.

11

Simmonds was on top. He ground his knee into Brenner's stomach and drove his fist at the hated face. It was as if he had been waiting for this all his life. He wanted to smash this man to a bloody pulp. But he was not quick enough. This man was like an eel. Simmonds' fist missed his face and scraped the rocky ground, sending a jet of pain to the deputy's shoulder. Then it was Brenner's turn to get his knee into Simmonds' stomach. He heaved upwards; and, with an agonized grunt, the deputy went flying backwards.

Simmonds' head hit a rock with a nasty crack and he was momentarily dazed. Through the haze he saw Brenner advancing on him. He could not see the hated face any more, but maybe that was only because the light was failing fast. He became sure that

Brenner must have a gun in his hand, that killer-light in his strange eyes, so it was with utter desperation that he flung himself upwards.

A blow glanced off the side of his head, spinning him half-round, yet not completely stopping his headlong charge. He tangled with Brenner, hugging him as if he were a long-lost brother. But the other man would not play: he got a crooked elbow beneath Simmonds' jaw and forced him backwards and Simmonds realized he was up against a tearing brutality as savage as his own.

One consolation was, however, that Brenner, too, seemed to have lost his gun. They were on even terms and that suited the deputy fine. He brought his knee up sharply and heard Brenner grunt, felt him wilt. Next moment they were apart, facing each other in the pass, which had suddenly gone dark. The echo of the horses' hooves had died. There was no sound except their own laboured breathing. They might have been the only two men left in the world, alone with nature, as it has been since the dawn of time, alone with their own hate and fury. Brenner limped slowly forward. Simmonds moved to one side so that he was away from the cluster of small rocks which were liable to trip him. The two men circled warily, getting their breath back, sizing each other up, watching for an opening.

Simmonds lunged with his right. Brenner blocked it, retaliated. Simmonds swerved. The two men were thrown together. Brenner's gimpy leg seemed suddenly to give way, but that was only because he had crouched. A powerful blow from Simmonds whistled over the other man's shoulder. Brenner drove a couple of blows to the deputy's stomach. Simmonds gulped and jack-knifed. But his stomach muscles were pretty hard and, instead of grabbing them with both hands, he had the presence of mind to keep his guard up, blocking Brenner's follow-up blow which, had it landed, might have broken his jaw.

Brenner followed up again with a regular flurry of blows and Simmonds could do little else but cover up and back, as he fought to regain his breath. His heels caught on a rock and he clawed wildly at the air as he felt himself falling. He twisted himself sideways and let his body go slack, a trick he had learned years ago when he had worked as a broncobuster in Texas. The rocks gave his hip a nasty jar, but he did not strike his head. He rolled as Brenner almost fell on top of him: the limping man had been carried forward so fast by the impetus of his attack that he had not been able to save himself.

Both men rolled away from the rocks, clawing at each other like a couple of spitting cats. Simmonds saw something glinting on the rock floor. His, or Brenner's, gun. He grabbed for it and missed. For a moment he had left himself wide open. A bunch of knuckles crashed into his mouth, bringing nausea and the salty taste of blood. He rolled and, in a daze, began to rise to his knees.

Brenner rose to his feet, backed off. He took in great gulps of air as he watched Simmonds, waited for him to rise. Simmonds was tottering to his feet when he saw the gun again. He dived for it.

Brenner was further away from it. Simmonds' hand closed over the butt and he lifted the gun. Brenner limped forward at surprising speed, kicked out with his good leg. His aim was bad. His foot missed Simmonds' gun-arm and bit into his other shoulder, knocking him backwards. The gun went off. Brenner clapped his hands to his face and staggered . . .

The world was spinning around him. The rocks were falling upon him from all sides, beating him down . . . down . . .

He struggled, but he could not fight off the rocks. They became suddenly soft. Soft, black and pulpy and they closed over him and there was no more pain and everything became black.

Jay Simmonds climbed to his feet. He looked a little stupidly at the gun in his hand. He wondered if he had meant to shoot Brenner. He did not think he had really: he had only wanted to bash him about and take him prisoner, take him back to town and make him talk. He (Simmonds) had been right after all — he'd tell the goddamned world! He was still a little dazed and his hip hurt him terribly where he had hit it on the rocks. Rats were gnawing at it. Large rats. His head felt as if it was going to burst. He raised his free hand. His wound had burst open again and blood had turned the sticking-plaster to a soggy mess.

Simmonds tried to fumble it back into place, but failed miserably. He only succeeded in plastering himself with blood. He was not sure whether the gun he held belonged to him or to Brenner. He stuck it into his holster and it fitted perfectly, so he figured it must be his own. He staggered across to Brenner and went down on one knee beside him. In the darkness Brenner's face seemed to be covered with blood. Also, he didn't seem to be breathing none.

Simmonds rose again. His head was beginning to clear a little. He staggered off down the trail to look for his horse. He found him around the next bend, contentedly trying to forage brown grass from between cracks in the rocks.

'Where's the other cayuse, my beauty?' said Simmonds.

The horse looked at him sideways, his eyes gleaming whitely in the dark.

Simmonds stroked his mane. 'I guess you wouldn't tell me if you knew,' he said inanely.

His voice sounded unnecessarily loud. The rocks threw its echo back to him. He shut his mouth tight, beginning to think that last blow on his head had addled his brains a little. He led the horse a little further along the trail. He even whistled a couple of times. But there was no sign of Brenner's mount. It must have gone completely haywire and bolted, taking its cargo with it.

Simmonds climbed on to his own horse. The slight exertion made his head spin so that he swayed in the saddle, almost fell off again. He had been tempted to ride on and look for the other horse, but now realized this would be a crazy thing to do. Out there was the desert. He must get back to Lagos and Doc Limpole or he was liable to become buzzard bait. Then again, there was Brenner: he might not be dead.

Simmonds went back and made another examination of his fallen foe. Somehow he did not hate the man quite so much now. He had fought well and, if it had not been for the lucky break of the gun, Simmonds had to admit to himself he might be the one lying there now.

There was little he could do here in the darkness. Grunting and sweating, fighting off nausea, he managed to get Brenner's body across the front of the saddle. He mounted behind it and urged his horse forward. He wondered whether old Josh was coming out with a posse. Perhaps he would meet them. Anyway, once he got out into the open where things could be seen, maybe he'd light a signal fire. Simmonds hunched in the saddle, tried to keep his eyes open as the horse swayed and jogged over the uneven rock surface. But finally they hit the plain and things were a little easier.

It seemed to take the horse ages to reach the rock outcrop they had passed on their way in. Maybe they were both crazy, him and the beast: maybe they had been going round in circles. Maybe he ought to stop, take a dram of water, light a fire, rest. If he kept on and did not meet anybody he was liable to topple from the saddle. Then both he and Brenner would be buzzard-bait for sure.

He made his decision and dismounted, ground-hitching his horse in the shelter of the rocks. He forced himself to keep on his pins. He found a flat rocky spot open in the direction of Lagos. He left his water-canteen standing there to mark the spot, then he went hunting firewood. Not until he had an armful of dry grass, dead cactus and other miscellaneous bits and pieces did he allow himself to take a short pull from the almost empty canteen.

He built the fire and then was horrified to discover he had no matches. He had left Brenner hanging over the front of the horse, but now lifted him down and rested him against the rocks. In Brenner's vest-pocket he found a box of lucifers. A few seconds later he had the fire blazing merrily. Then he went off to forage for more fuel.

★ ★ ★

Tom Brenner had been aware of a bumping, swaying motion beneath him. It was like the motion of a boat on a choppy swell. He was a plainsman, he had not had much truck with boats. He had been in a riverboat smash once down in St Louis and had tried to swim. But cowboys are not used to swimming and he would have drowned if he had not been picked up by two men in a small rowing-boat. He had lain in the bottom of the boat, in the blackness, full of a rocking nausea.

Seemed like he was back in that time now. He became panicky and tried to struggle upwards. But, although his brain flashed urgent commands to his limbs, his limbs would not obey. The sickness spread from his body to his head, and his head was swelling enormously, it was his head that was keeping him down.

It was only gradually that full awareness came to him. It was his sense of smell that gave him the final solution to this nauseating, rocking problem. There was a pungent smell in his nostrils, a familiar smell that was not so pleasant at close quarters as it had once been. He discovered finally that this was mainly due to the fact that he had a chunk of horse's mane in his mouth.

He spat cautiously and managed to remove the impediment. He fought back rising nausea. He felt the rider above him move and he went deathly still, hoping he was not going to be sick. But that feeling passed — though his head bobbed up and down hugely like an over-ripe pumpkin. He thought that, if he tried to fix his mind on something, he would forget his troubles. He was not dying — yet.

He tried to figure out his position on the horse. He had been slung across in front of the saddle like a sack of meal, but his head was at a crooked angle, that was how he had gotten a mouthful of mane. The horse's damp, smelly flanks were rubbing against his face now with the rocking motion of his progress. When this progress, which had begun to lull him, suddenly ceased, it was as if he had been kicked in the stomach. He almost blacked out.

He felt the rider climb down from the saddle and his interest in this movement and what might happen next helped him to hold on to his wits. Also, things were coming back to him pretty fast now and he remembered who the rider was.

He lay still and heard the rider move away from him, heard the horse's jaws munching rhythmically as he picked at dry grass.

Brenner raised his head a little. At first it felt as if the sky had fallen on it. The stars were very hot and had sharp points. But he persevered and finally he could see a little way ahead of him in the darkness. He was relieved to discover he was facing in the right direction. He spotted the vague bulk of Jay Simmonds, then he subsided again as the deputy came towards him.

Next moment hands grasped him and he was dragged from the horse and propped against a rock. This rough treatment made him feel so ill that he could not have done anything about it if he had tried. Neither could he prevent Simmonds rummaging in his pockets and stealing his matches. Maybe the big fancy galoot thought he had a dead man on his hands.

Simmonds moved away again and Brenner fought his weakness until he got things into perspective again. He saw the fire blaze and he watched Simmonds move away from it to gather more wood. He paid particular attention to the gun in Simmonds' holster and, as he waited for the man to strut nearer, called upon all his reserves of energy not to let him down when the final effort became necessary.

Simmonds stopped a few yards away, and stooped to pick up a stick. Brenner uncoiled himself and sprang. Pain screamed through his body, but his hand closed over the gun and he pulled it from its holster. He rolled and came up on one elbow.

Simmonds stared in amazement into the muzzle of the gun. Brenner began to rise to his feet. Simmonds began to get over his initial stupefaction and watched closely, moved a couple of steps nearer. Brenner jerked the gun meaningfully. He was on his feet now, but his gimpy leg gave way.

Simmonds rushed this walking dead man. Brenner dragged another reserve of strength from somewhere. He backed a couple of steps almost nimbly and lashed out with the gun. The barrel caught the deputy neatly across the side of the head. With a groan, he crumpled; then pitched forward on his face at Brenner's feet.

The gun in his hand, Brenner bent over the prostrate form. Simmonds lay on his face; but the firelight illuminated the face of the man above him, red-splashed like a scalp-hunting Indian brave's, the lips drawn back from the white teeth, the eyes glaring.

The head was cocked on one side suddenly in an attitude of listening. Then Brenner got down on his knees and pressed his ear to the ground. He swayed a little when he rose again, he felt giddy. The sound was carried to him now on the evening breeze and, though vague, was unmistakable. The humming of horses' hooves; and quite a sizeable party of horsemen at that.

He looked down at the supine form of Jay Simmonds. He hefted the gun in his hand. 'I ought to kill you,' he said from between clenched teeth. But he dropped the gun into his holster and turned and limped over to Simmonds' horse and mounted it.

A few seconds later he was riding at breakneck speed through the pass, holding on like grim death, swaying in the saddle. He had begun to get giddy again. He had the feeling that his head had swollen to three times its normal size, so that a large part of it was hollow and if he did not hold on tight with arms and legs, the wind in the pass would carry him away. He knew he was supposed to be looking for something — but he had forgotten what. He might have been out on the flat somewhere when he finally tumbled from the horse's back, but by that time he was not aware of anything any more.

12

Things came back to him pretty quickly when he came to. Maybe the enforced period of unconsciousness had served to unscramble his wits. He had expected to find himself lying on the hard rocky surface of the pass. He moved his limbs experimentally and was a little surprised to discover that there was nothing broken. His head ached abominably, but was back to normal size. He was lying on something soft which did not hurt when he moved. There was blackness all around him.

He felt for his gun. It had gone and his belt with it. His trousers bagged at the waist. He wriggled his toes. Somebody had taken his socks off, and the kerchief from around his neck, and his leather vest. His shirt was open down the front and a faint draft chilled his bare chest. He took his time over fastening all his buttons, getting rational at the same time. Then when it was done, he began to feel around him with his hands. It did not take him long to discover that he was lying on a wall-bunk, the kind that was found in ranch bunkhouses.

He swung himself outward and felt for the floor with his feet. He made that all right, but had to sit awhile till his head settled back into its normal position. His eyes were getting accustomed to the darkness now, and he had figured out he was in some kind of room or cabin. He was rising slowly to his feet when he heard the footsteps. Next moment the door had opened and a tall figure passed through it. Brenner let himself fall back into a sitting position on the bunk. No matter which way you looked at it, he was a sitting duck.

The door had closed again and he saw the tall figure only dimly now. It crossed the room unerringly, as if it knew its way around pretty well. A match scratched and Brenner blinked in the light as a hurricane lamp was lit on a small table.

The tall figure turned and looked at him. It was that of an old man so thin and gnarled that he looked as tall and ageless as a tree. His clean-shaven monkey-like face was a net of wrinkles, from which bright blue eyes peered. In the crook of his arm was a rifle, but it did not seem to be pointing at anything in particular.

'Oh, so you've come out of it, son,' he said.

'I have. Where am I?'

'You're quite safe from whatever was chasing you, if that's what you mean. This cabin belonged to old Charlie Bennett. I'm one of the few people who know of it.'

'I knew Charlie Bennett.'

'Very many people knew Charlie Bennett,' said the old man gravely. 'He was a very popular fellow was Charlie. Do you feel like you could eat somethin', younker?'

'Yes, I do.'

'All right. Eat first, talk afterwards. You just lie back and take it easy while I fix something.'

Brenner was glad to take the old man's advice. The cabin was beginning to spin around him. He lay back on the bunk.

'We'll get something inside you first,' said the old-timer. 'Then we'll take a look at that haid. My name's Rory Jones.'

'Glad to know you, Mr Jones. Mine's Brenner — Tom Brenner.'

'Got to get some more wood for the stove, Mr Brenner,' said Rory Jones, and stepped out of the cabin once more.

The door closed behind him. Then it opened again and the monkey-face and white head was popped round the corner. 'There are some cigarettes on that cupboard within reach of your hand. Help yourself.'

'Thanks,' said Brenner. But the door

had already closed again.

He twisted his head and saw the oblong cardboard box of store cigarettes. There did not seem to be any matches, but when he reached for the box and opened it he discovered there were matches inside, too. He struck one, lit up. The first drag made him light-headed, his stomach grumble; he realized he needed food and drink far more than he needed Lady Nicotine. He dropped the cigarette on the floor then swung from the bunk once more and poked the glowing ash gingerly with his bare feet until all heat had gone from it.

He fought rising nausea. He heard Rory Jones returning and, because he did not wish the old man to see him in his weakness, he lay back once more. He lay and looked at the log ceiling and listened to the old man busying himself at the stove. Judging by Rory's language, the fire had gone out. But that was eventually remedied and Brenner heard the fire roaring in the stove-pipe, followed in double-quick time by the clink of pans, the smell of coffee and baking beans.

'You awake, son?' asked Rory suddenly.

'Yeh.'

'Your haid hurt now?'

'No. But my stomach's kinda clamouring.'

'We'll soon fix that,' chuckled the old man.

Brenner straightened up again. A fellow simply couldn't act like a dying duck when there was an old buzzard like Rory to liven him up. The old man was placing hot, appetising food and drink on the small table. Brenner rested one tentative foot on the floor, then another. He was pleased to discover he could walk without his head falling off. He made it to the table and let himself fall on to a nearby chair.

Rory gazed at him with eyes that seemed to twinkle with some secret joke. 'I would've brought it across to you,' he said.

'I've still got two pins,' said Brenner wryly. 'An' they're younger than yours are.'

'I figured you weren't the kind of younker who'd let a leetle knock on the head faze him,' said Rory.

Brenner could not answer that one because he had his mouth full of beans. Rory set-to also, and for a time neither of them could find room for conversation. Brenner was thinking the old man did not seem in a hurry to ask questions. So, when he began to feel better, he asked one for himself.

'Did you know Charlie Bennett was dead?'

'Yes, I know. News travels fast in this territory. As a matter of fact, I was making my way to Lagos to pay my last respects to Charlie when my horse went lame and I had to hole up here. Were you at the funeral, son?'

'Wal, I was in Lagos at the time, but not actually at the funeral.'

'Mebbe you better tell me all about it,' said the old man gruffly. 'You see, I found the horse with the dead man across it and the burlap sack full of money.'

'What makes you think a dead man and a sack full of money would have something to do with me?'

The old man shrugged. 'I put two an' two together an' made four. Could be just coincidence, of course . . . '

The voice tailed off, and a thin smile crossed Brenner's face. 'All right,' he said. 'But first let me get a cigarette.'

'Sure,' said Rory Jones. 'Sure. Help yourself.' But there was a wariness in his voice now that had not been there before.

★   ★   ★

Brenner took his time in lighting the cigarette and getting it to draw well. He wanted to get things straight in his mind before he spoke of them. So many things had happened. He did not return to the table, but sat on the edge of the bunk again. He wanted to watch Rory's

169

reaction as the story was unfolded. The old man had the inside edge.

He began by telling of another old man, found dead in the desert with four bullets in him. The story, as it progressed, was like a brutal fairy-tale, but Brenner could not judge by Rory's demeanour whether the old man suspected it of being only such a tale.

Incidents, though perilous, had been pretty elemental and clearcut until the girl came into the story. So Brenner made little mention of the girl, or of the effect she had had upon him.

He remembered the last time he had seen her and the way, a little disturbed, he had gone back to the window after she left him. He had peered through the dusty glass, a cigarette burning away in his hand.

★　★　★

It was hard for him to determine how long he had been at the window before he spotted the man.

The *hombre*, acting in a very shifty and suspicious manner, was leading a horse among the ash cans and miscellaneous junk in back of the Main Street establishments.

Brenner had to crane his neck at a tortuous angle in order to follow the progress of the man and horse. Then they stopped, Brenner could not see the man's face, but saw him take a black kerchief from his pocket, lift it. Then both man and horse passed from sight.

Brenner hesitated only a fraction, looking round the room as if he thought something was missing. Then he sat on the edge of the bed and quickly put on his boots. A few seconds later he was running across the floor of the undertaking parlour, still looking around him in a puzzled sort of way. He did not have a gun. He felt half naked.

He heard the single shot outside and wasted no more time, but flung open the alley door and ran for the stables. There was one horse there; a saddle hung on the wall nearby. Even as

Brenner saddled the beast he could hear the hooves of the hold-up man's mount fading away in the distance. Brenner mounted and urged the horse to the back of the buildings, knowing this was the quickest way out of town. When he hit the trail, his quarry was merely a puff of dust far ahead.

Brenner did not know whose horse he had commandeered, but the beast was fast. He was a big chestnut with a headstrong way, powerful muscles surged and vibrated, he had a rhythmic sway that carried him over the ground at an enormous rate.

The early afternoon sun was at its most brassy brilliance, and Brenner discovered that staring after his quarry only made his eyes run. He bent over the flowing mane and gave the beast his head. The breeze was whipped into a wind, blustering past him. It was good to be free again, and with the promise of action ahead. For a moment he almost forgot he was unarmed. In any case, that was something he could stop thinking about until he caught up with his quarry. He figured that, unless this magnificent beast put his foot in a gopher hole and crippled both himself and his rider, he had a good chance of catching the hold-up man.

He looked back once and was surprised to see how far already he had travelled from town. Lagos looked like a cluster of child's bricks tossed down higgledy-piggledy in this sun-blistered immensity.

And when he raised his head again, it was to look onwards to the foothills, shimmering like blue intangible things. But they vere nearer now, much nearer. Soon they began to assume concrete shape. And then he saw, more clearly, too, the rider approach them and, a few seconds later, disappear amongst them. The trail was still there, beaten down; the hold-up man was taking the main pass. Brenner remembered it, its craggy sides, the outcrops which dotted its length. So many places which seemed to be designed exclusively for the use of a cunning drygulch merchant. So, when he entered the pass himself, he slowed his horse to a walk and listened. And not until he could hear the sound of racing hooves echoing up ahead did he push on at breakneck speed.

He had been going so fast and he came in clear sight of the man so suddenly that it surprised both of them. The man took out his gun and fired, but the slug went wild.

Brenner saw his face, plump, red, with little evil eyes. Then, as the gun was lifted again, Brenner ducked and heard the slug whistle over his head.

Gunshots did not seem to throw a cramp in the big chestnut's stride; he literally surged forward.

Brenner swung himself sideways and leapt from the saddle. Another slug almost parted his hair; then he had hold of the other man and they were falling together.

They crashed on to the rock floor in a wild tangle of arms and legs. Brenner gulped as a bony knee was driven into his stomach. An elbow was rammed against his throat and he was rolled over on his back. His opponent was mighty strong. Brenner let himself go limp and the man came down on top of him like a sack of sand. Then it was Brenner's turn to use both knees, and his feet, propelling the man upwards, driving his fists into the red, strained face. The face was bleeding; then it was not there any more and Brenner rose to a sitting position. The other man had been flung against the rocks; Brenner jack-knifed upwards and flung himself after him. A flying boot narrowly missed Brenner's chin. Another one jolted his shoulder, stopping him almost in mid-air. The two men fell apart again, tumbling grotesquely, glaring at each other.

The bandit had dropped his gun, but now it lay near him. Even as Brenner saw it, the man spotted it, too. As the *hombre*'s hand closed over the butt of the weapon, Brenner flung himself forward like a wildcat.

The gun went off, but the slug whined and ricocheted harmlessly away among the rocks. The two men rose upwards, taut, straining; grappling for the gun. The bandit cried out with pain as Brenner jerked his arm back. The gun shot upwards, loose, like a cork from a bottle. It hit the rocks and went off again, the slug zipping savagely between the two men, almost taking the bandit's nose off.

The man jerked his head back with the shock and his grip on Brenner relaxed. Brenner drove two terrific blows to the contorted face. Blood spurted. The man went back against a boulder, which held him. He tried to cover up, but Brenner beat down his guard with savage strength. He drove his fists again and again into that face until it dissolved in blood; blood was a mist in front of Brenner's eyes, he groped again for this hated enemy . . . But the bandit, despite the beating he had taken, still had some life in him. He kicked out. The heavy toecap seemed to explode on Brenner's leg. His gimpy one. Pain jetted upwards, spread over Brenner's body like jetting flames. Brenner fell forward on top of the man. He saw the face through a red mist. He felt for the hated throat and found it and pressed.

Finger-nails tore at his hands. Knees and feet drummed at him. He hardly felt them; he kept pressing, pressing, while the blood drummed in his ears and a red mist floated before his eyes.

Red . . . red . . . everything was red, going slowly dark, useless, until it seemed like there was nothing to hold on to anymore . . .

'You strangled him,' said Rory Jones softly. 'He wasn't a pretty sight.'

Brenner nodded his head slowly. His expression was a little bemused, as if he was still reliving the incident.

'What did you do then?' probed Rory softly.

'I picked up the man's gun,' said Brenner tonelessly. 'I didn't have a gun you see. But this one was no good. It had gotten smashed on the rocks. If I had tried to fire it, I should've probably blown my hand off. I threw it away. The man's horse had wandered off, but my chestnut was still there. I put the body and the bank money across the saddle an' mounted up an' started back for Lagos. In the pass I ran into Jay Simmonds, hot on the trail. He didn't give me a chance to tell him anything. I don't even think he noticed the dead body across my saddle. He was after my blood all right.'

'Jay allus seems to be after somebody's blood,' said Rory drily.

So Brenner went on to tell him of his fight with the deputy and of its outcome.

When he had finished, the old man said with a chuckle, 'You're suttinly a glutton for punishment, Mr Brenner. As I remember Jay Simmonds, he's no puffball.'

'He almost did for me,' said Brenner grimly. 'An' I guess if you hadn't picked me up I'd be buzzard bait now. I'm mighty obliged to you, Mr Jones.'

'Don't mention it, Mr Brenner.' The old man's bright blue eyes crinkled with silent laughter. The network of wrinkles upon his weather-beaten face became more tortuous than ever. Seemed like there was a sort of affinity between this old desert-rat and the young man with the gimpy leg and the old eyes.

13

'How about this buzzard outside?' went on Rory. 'We ought to bury him. He's beginning to stink.'

'He's evidence,' said Brenner.

'Evidence that you didn't stick up the bank, huh?'

'Yeh.'

'But you still don't have evidence that you didn't kill Charlie Bennett.'

'Do you think I need evidence for that?'

'Not for me you don't. But other people . . . ' Rory let his sentence tail off, shrugged his shoulders.

'Thanks, old-timer.'

'Shucks,' Rory rose decisively. 'Let me fix that head o' yourn.'

He crossed the room and delved in a small wall-cupboard and brought forth bandages and a box of salve.

'Old Charlie was a mighty nice an'

tidy person,' he said. 'What kind of skunk would want to kill him?'

'Some people will kill an' keep on killin' for gold,' said Brenner. 'If Charlie had made a haul,' he spread his hands, 'well, there's your motive.'

'I guess it could've been that dead buzzard outside.'

'Could've, I guess. That'd be the simplest solution, wouldn't it?'

'The simplest solutions are often the right ones,' said Rory. He put the old iron kettle on top of the stove. 'Better get that haid bathed first, young feller.'

And a few minutes later this was being done, followed by salving and bandaging by Rory's gnarled, but surprisingly gentle, bands.

'That ain't gonna slow you up none,' said the old man.

Brenner stood up. 'Thanks, Rory,' he said. 'I feel better already. I guess I better get moving now. If I don't miss my guess, the posse's already on the rampage. Mebbe I'll meet 'em.'

'Yeh, an' mebbe they'll start shootin'

first an' asking questions afterwards, like Jay Simmonds did. I guess they picked him up, huh?'

'I guess they did. I guess that was them I heard riding up when I left Simmonds.'

'I'll ride in with you,' said Rory. 'They won't fire on me. An' I can substantiate your story about the hold-up man an' the money.'

'You don't have to, Rory. You've done enough. I . . . '

'I was on my way to Lagos in any case, wasn't I?' interrupted the old man, with assumed ferocity. 'Let's have no more argument. I'm coming with you.'

'All right, don't get your dander up.' Brenner put his head on one side. 'What did happen to that bank money anyway?'

'Well, you see, I'd got everythin' planned. I buried the money in some rocks back o' the cabin.' Rory jerked a hoary thumb. His face was as grave as a judge's, his fierce eyebrows hid his eyes.

'Then I aimed to get rid o' you painlessly, bury you an' your dead friend an' light out for places unknown. But you seemed such a nice young feller that I didn't have the heart to do it.'

Rory slapped his knees with his hands and began to chortle. Brenner's thin smile turned into a grin. Then he began to laugh, too. The sound seemed to come from deep down in his stomach, as if it had been buried there for a long time.

His broad shoulders still quaking, he turned towards the door. 'Come on. Let's get that stiff prepared for the journey.'

Both men passed outside. 'It was true what I told you,' said Rory. 'The part about the money, anyway. I did hide it the back of the shack. I'll go an' get it.' He pointed. 'The hosses are over there. See that cleft?'

Brenner peered forward. Dimly in the pale moonlight he could see the black slash against the rock.

'Yeh,' he said, and strode forward.

He was almost at the place when a slug buzzed past his ear like an angry hornet. The whiplash report of a rifle awoke the echoes. He threw himself flat and rolled, his hand instinctively going to his hip. No gun, of course. He cursed softly, looking about him. Probably the unseen marksman was only waiting for him to move again. He was in shadow where he lay, but to reach the cleft, which was his objective, he had to cross a wide slash of moonlight-bathed rock-face.

Without moving his head any more than was necessary, he looked behind him. Much of the shadow came from a cluster of rocks to the right of him. He looked up at the rocks where the shot had come from. All he could see was blackness. He twisted, flung himself sideways, rolled into the cover of the rocks. There was no more shooting.

He looked back at the cabin. He could not see Rory anywhere. He calculated the distance with his eye.

Hundred and fifty yards; maybe more. Moonlight and shadow pretty evenly broken up. If he could get around the corner of the cabin, the corner behind which Rory had gone, he would be out of line of the marksman. Unless the *hombre* had shifted, of course: maybe that was his reason for not opening up again: maybe he was moving, finding a more comfortable spot from which to continue with his turkey-shoot.

Brenner made his decision and acted upon it immediately. He darted forward, ran, half-crouching. Another slug kicked up dust at his heels just before he reached the corner of the cabin. There were answering shots, but from the other direction: Brenner heard the slugs go over his head. Next moment he was rolling in cover beside old Rory, who had a rifle to his shoulder.

'Thanks, old-timer,' he panted. He stabbed a finger at the rifle. 'How did you get that?'

Rory grinned and jerked a thumb behind him. Brenner saw that the tiny side window of the cabin was open. 'All I had to do was put my arm in.'

'The place's lit up like a Christmas tree,' said Brenner.

'We're in shadow here an' if that sniper changes his position, we can easily get back behind the cabin an' keep that money company.'

'Mebbe that's what the sniper's after.'

'Mebbe. One thing I am pretty sure he is after though, an' that's your blood.'

'Yeh, he almost had it, too.'

'I've only got one rifle,' said Rory. 'But take this.' He took his old Frontier Colt from its holster and handed it over.

The two men stood shoulder to shoulder and leaned a little. Up above them the rocks were black and diminutive. The only sound was the faint soughing of the night breezes.

*　*　*

It was indeed the galloping posse that Brenner had heard when he left the unconscious Jay Simmonds. The fugitive was riding through the pass when the ten riders clustered in the firelight around the motionless form.

Sheriff Penrose dropped from his horse and went down beside his deputy. 'He ain't dead,' he said.

Jay groaned and tried to sit up. Old Josh put his arm around the younger man's shoulder and helped him into a sitting position.

'The murderin' skunk got away,' were the first words Simmonds said. Then his voice rose almost hysterically. 'What are you all standing around for? Let's get after him.'

'You're doing no more riding tonight, younker,' Josh told him. The sheriff half-rose, looked about him.

'Caspar, will you have Jay on the front of your horse?'

'Sure.'

Simmonds, expostulating weakly, was helped on to the mount belonging to the crippled youth. Caspar climbed up behind.

'You go with 'em, Cal,' said the sheriff, turning to the hare-lipped old-timer, Happy Cal.

'Go with them where?'

'Back to town, you jackass. See that Jay gets to Doc Limpole right away.'

'Aw, Josh, I wanted to . . . '

'Don't argue. Do you want Jay to bleed to death?' There was little danger that this would happen, but the possibility seemed to alarm Cal into acquiescence. 'Oh, all right,' he growled.

Young Caspar had not said another word. Whether he wanted to stay with the hunt or not, he was obeying orders. The little cavalcade passed on into the night in the direction of Lagos. One of the men was stamping out the red embers of the fire. 'All right,' said Josh Penrose. 'Let's get after that skunk.'

Everybody remounted and, a few seconds later, the band swept on through the pass. They were getting to the other end when Josh gave the word to slow down. 'He might be hiding out.

We don't want to miss him. Spread out a little.'

'Looks like he's heading for the desert,' said fat Coney.

'Wait a minute,' put in Bern Cantell. 'I thought I heard something.'

'You're imagining things,' said Lemmy Dricourt.

'No,' said Bern decisively. 'I heard a horse nicker. I think I've got an idea where it's coming from, too.' He looked interrogatively towards the lean figure of Josh Penrose.

The sheriff said, 'Go ahead, Bern. Lead the way.'

The undertaker urged his horse to the forefront. 'There's a cleft in the rocks up ahead,' he said softly. 'It looks like a dead end — but it isn't. Go carefully an' don't make any more noise than you can help.'

He rode a little way ahead and suddenly disappeared from view. When the rest of the riders reached the spot they could see the black slash of the cleft and the ghostly outline of horse and rider against it. Bern led the way.

After climbing for a while they reached a wide ledge. The undertaker said, 'I think we had better leave our horses here. There are too many of them for safe climbing. We'll go the rest of the way on foot. We'll spread out a little so we shan't get in each other's way.'

He led the way again, climbing nimbly. He was an active man for his age. Sheriff Penrose ran him a close second. The rest of the bunch spread out behind, with the two heavyweights, fat Coney and huge Lemmy, bringing up the rear. Finally Bern held up his hand to call a halt. He went down on his belly behind a cluster of boulders. The sheriff joined him and they looked down on a tiny moonwashed valley with a lamplit cabin in the centre of it. There was silence down there. Nothing moved. The sheriff called the other men on and they clustered along the ridge.

The sheriff opened his mouth to speak to Bern Cantell, then it closed again when the undertaker's bony grip closed over his arm.

Two men had come out of the cabin. One went round the back of it; the other came on across the clearing. 'That's Brenner,' hissed Josh. 'I couldn't see the other one properly. I couldn't figure him. But that's Brenner all right — you can tell by his limp.'

'I'm not sure who the other one was,' said Bern. 'Maybe . . . '

The rest of his sentence was drowned by the crash of a shot. The little figure down below hit the ground, rolling. Fat Coney had his rifle to his shoulder.

'Hold it!' snarled the sheriff. 'If you hadn't pulled that we might've got down and took him quietly. We want him to talk . . . '

'Hell, you didn't even hit him,' said one of the other men disgustedly. 'He's taken cover.' His voice rose excitedly. 'Look, the skunk's running for it.'

'All right, Coney,' said the sheriff unemotionally. 'Try an' get him in the leg. In the leg you understand!'

Coney nodded, sighted, squeezed trigger. He was a good marksman, but the range was bad and the light not good. Brenner disappeared in the shadows at the side of the cabin. A rifle cracked down there. The slug smacked viciously into the rock-face above the heads of the posse.

The echoes rolled away and died. Nothing moved down below now.

'Can we get down there, Bern?' asked the sheriff.

'Yes. But we'll have to expose ourselves now and then. The best thing to do is plant a couple of men up here with rifles to keep Brenner and his friend pinned down.'

Josh nodded, crawled a little way. He conferred with Lemmy Dricourt and Coney, then gave instructions to the other men. He rejoined Bern. 'Lemmy an' Coney will stay an' keep us covered.'

'All right, let's go,' said Bern Cantell, and led the way.

'Tell me,' said Josh in his ear. 'What

is this place. How did you get to know about it?'

'Didn't you know about it?'

'Should I?'

'No, maybe not. This was Charlie Bennett's retreat from the world. I think he kept it secret even from his friends. I came upon it by accident one day when I was out riding. Charlie was here. He gave me a royal welcome, but told me not to talk about it.'

'Well, I was one of Charlie's friends, too, but this is news to me. I always thought Charlie bedded down under the stars, wherever he happened to be.'

'He did. But I think this was his retreat when he got a little fed up with the world,' said Bern succinctly. 'I guess we've all got some kind of retreat, though it doesn't always take such a concrete form as Charlie's.'

'It shore is a dandy hideout,' said Josh. 'I wonder how Brenner came to find it.'

14

It was a silent trio that rode back to Lagos on two horses. Happy Cal was brooding over the action he might be missing while he was playing wet-nurse to a wounded man: a wounded man of whom he wasn't particularly fond at that. Jay Simmonds was still groggy; and maybe he was brooding also. Young Caspar was a pretty silent character at the best of times and maybe he, too, regretted the way the night had petered out for old Cal and himself.

It was late when they reached the edge of town. 'I guess Doc Limpole will be in — if nobody didn't get shot tonight,' said Happy Cal.

'I don't want to see any sawbones,' grumbled Simmonds.

'Sheriff's orders,' said Cal. He grabbed the bridle of Caspar's mount.

'Yeh, we better do what the sheriff

ordered,' said Caspar.

'Thought you'd gone dumb, younker,' chortled Happy Cal. A few seconds later he halted the cavalcade outside the doctor's house. A light shone in one of the upstairs windows.

'Can you walk?' said Cal.

'Course I can walk,' retorted Simmonds, aquiescent now, but still disgruntled.

He allowed Cal and Caspar to escort him to the doc's porch. Cal hammered on the door.

A window was flung open up above and the familiar querulous voice yelled, 'What in tarnation is all the shindig about?'

'We got a wounded man here, doc,' carolled the harelipped old-timer. 'Deppity Simmonds. He got knocked on the haid. Addled his brains a mite, I reckin.'

Simmonds swore at the grinning old-timer. The window slammed up above. The listeners followed the doc's noisy progress downstairs until he opened the door. An ankle-length blue and white striped nightshirt was revealed below

195

the shabby dressing gown and above the battered moccasins. The doc looked like a lean, ancient and querulous owl.

'Well, don't just stand there. Bring him in.'

Cal and Caspar took an elbow each, but Simmonds shook their hands away. 'I ain't crippled,' he said, which was maybe not a very tactful remark to make in front of Caspar.

The crippled youth stepped back. He stayed behind on the porch while Cal ushered Simmonds inside. The doc left the door wide open, but Caspar made no attempt to enter. He stood on the porch and gazed out into the darkness. There was a tortured look on his thin face, a look that turned him old beyond his years, older than even his frailty could have made him, an oldness of the soul older than tortured men.

He was still standing there motionless when his two companions came out. Simmonds' head was bandaged and he walked with his old arrogant stride.

'We've had a drink, Caspar,' said old Cal. 'Doc wants to know if you need one.'

The medico came to the doorway. Caspar turned towards him, the lamplight striking his face. 'No, thanks, doc,' he said, and led the way to the horses.

Doc Limpole stood on his porch and watched the cavalcade move away. Simmonds was walking now, holding on to the bridle of Caspar's horse. The deputy was pretty tough: he'd live to a ripe old age if somebody didn't kick his head in first. It was not Simmonds that the doctor was worrying about now, it was the other young man. Caspar had looked mighty sick — sicker than he had ever looked before.

Simmonds quit the other two at their lodging-house. 'I'm goin' on to the jail. I'll doss down there till morning.' He was better-tempered now. He even thanked them for helping him into town.

'Don't mention it,' said Cal.

Caspar said nothing. They trailed off.

Simmonds walked on towards the jail. He looked back once to see Caspar gazing after him. Then the youth disappeared up the alley beside the lodging-house.

Simmonds shook his head from side to side. Queer sort of gink, that Caspar.

There was a light still on in the undertaking parlour. Downstairs, too. The deputy paused in his stride. Bern was out with the posse; Louise would be alone, probably sitting up waiting for her father. He turned towards the place, then changed his mind and ploughed on. His head was beginning to throb again. He figured he was not exactly a pretty sight either.

He reached the jail house and let himself in and went straight into the back place to clean himself up. He had his face buried in a towel when there was a knock on the outer door. He dried himself hastily. On his way through he took a gun from the desk drawer and made sure it was loaded. It was in his hand when he opened the door. But he lowered the weapon when he saw who his visitor was.

'I saw you go by,' said Louise Cantell. 'Are you hurt?'

Simmonds' heart leapt and, with that, a lot of his arrogance left him. 'I just got knocked on the head. Nothing to worry about. C'mon inside, Louise.'

The girl preceded him into the lamplit office. 'Where are the rest of the posse?' she asked.

'They're still tailing Brenner.'

'They haven't caught him yet?'

'They hadn't when I left them.'

'He stayed in our loft,' said the girl. 'I've been tidying it out. It found me something to do while I'm waiting. I found this down the back of the bed — it must've fallen out of his pocket or something. I — I thought the sheriff ought to see it — it might help you in your investigations.'

Simmonds looked at the girl a little strangely as he took the small folder from her. Its cover was of leather, but so battered and dirty that its original colour was indeterminate. But Jay Simmonds knew what that colour had been. Blue! And whoever the folder belonged to had fought in the Civil War, as Simmonds himself had.

He opened the folder and read aloud. 'Captain Tom Bennett . . . *Bennett!*' he repeated.

'You know him?' said the girl.

But Simmonds was staring into space and when he did answer it was as if he was talking to himself. 'No wonder he puzzled me — no wonder he looked familiar. If he had used his right name, I should've known who he was right away. He was in the brother-company to mine at Chatta-nooga. He was the youngest officer in the bunch. He got a couple of medals as well as a silver kneecap in place of the one he got smashed by grape-shot. Everybody had heard of Tom Bennett . . . '

'And they kept hearing about him afterwards,' said Louise, tonelessly. 'Tom Bennett, the young marshal of

San Antone, the fastest gun in the West.'

'A lawman's got to be fast,' said Simmonds. He scratched his head and, for a moment, looked almost boyish. 'An' to think I almost threw down on him. I'm lucky to be alive.'

'Yes, he's a killer, isn't he?' The girl's voice was utterly emotionless. 'He's got quite a notorious reputation.'

'He did have. But I heard he'd left San Antone about twelve months ago. He dropped completely out of sight. Mebbe he'd got a little tired of all the shootin' an' fightin' a famous lawman would have to do in a hotspot like San Antone. There's always some drunken cowpoke tryin' to find out how fast the famous gunman really is. Mebbe that was why Tom Bennett was travellin' incognito.'

'I thought he was your enemy. Now you seem to be sticking up for him.'

Simmonds' eyes widened. 'Yeh, I do — don't I?'

'Because we know who he is now,

does that make him innocent of the crimes he's been suspected of?'

'No-o, I guess not. Though those crimes seem out of calibre for a man of Tom Bennett's sort. What did you think when you found this folder, the kind of folder any man would be proud to own?'

Simmonds' clever thrust went home. The girl flushed. She began suddenly to like the florid deputy. His arrogance seemed to have left him. His hate of Tom Brenner had been purged from him with this new revelation. Now he was being scrupulously fair. She could do no more than be fair herself before him, even though she would have to reveal some of the things that were in her innermost heart, some of things that of late she had been trying to hide even from herself.

She said: 'When I saw the name on the folder, I wondered if Tom was any relation to old Charlie Bennett. If he was, that seemed to put a new light on everything. All along I couldn't believe that, although he had killed, as men have to sometimes in these lawless places, he couldn't be guilty of horrible, cowardly crimes.'

'You were kinda taken by him, weren't you, Louise?' said Simmonds softly.

She was aware of his own regard for her and she knew what it must have cost him to speak those words. She realized the depth of this man, which his arrogance and pugnacity must have hidden from so many people besides herself. Such a forthright question could only bring forth the same kind of answer. She said:

'Yes, I suppose I *was* taken by him, Jay.'

Simmonds tapped the battered leather folder on his knuckles. 'Josh will have to see this. I'll ride out an' see if I can catch the posse.'

'I'll come with you.'

'No, Louise. There's no need. You can trust me.'

'I know that, Jay. But I want to come.

My father's out there, too, you know.'

The man shrugged. 'I can't force you to stay.'

'I'll go and saddle my horse and get ready.'

'All right. I'll pick you up by your place.'

'Yes,' she said, and ran from the office.

Simmonds worked swiftly. He went out and saddled the spare horse in the jail house stable and led the beast out front.

He entered the office again and stopped dead on the threshold.

Caspar sat on the edge of the desk. In his hand was a gun which looked far too large for the bony white knuckles which gripped it. The muzzle was pointed quite steadily at the deputy's chest.

'I came in the back way while you were out there,' said Caspar in a strange, toneless kind of voice. 'My horse's out there. I slipped away from the lodging-house without Cal knowing. I had to tell somebody before I left town.'

'Tell somebody what?' Simmonds realized he was dealing with somebody who was not quite normal. He could go for his gun, but he did not think he would make it. He made his voice as flat and unemotional as possible to match Caspar's own tones. Then he waited.

Finally Caspar said, 'I killed Charlie Bennett an' took his dust. I've been sorry for it ever since. I felt if I didn't tell somebody about it soon, I'd go mad. I didn't tell Cal because that might've caused me to have had to shoot him, too, and I didn't want to do that. Cal has been mighty nice to me. I ain't sorry I killed a man, but I was sorry it was old Charlie. I liked old Charlie . . .'

The voice tailed off. The eyes seemed to be staring right through Simmonds, but the gun was still as steady as a rock.

'Why did you kill old Charlie, Caspar?' asked the deputy quietly.

'I didn't mean to. I was out riding. I often go out riding. Nobody knows that, I guess, except Cal. Nobody here cares what I do. I could die on the street like a dog and nobody would bother . . . '

'That's not true, Caspar. There are some mighty nice people in Lagos. You don't have to take any notice of the drunks and riff-raff. You're just imagining things.'

The youth's eyes flamed. 'Don't say that! I don't imagine things! I've seen people laughing at me.'

Simmonds realized he would have to go easy if he wanted to live to hear the rest of the story. He had never laughed at this boy himself, had only been indifferent to him, thinking him a moody young cuss. Now he could not even be angry with him — he was tired of being angry with people — he could only feel pity, knowing that he would have to kill Caspar if he had the chance, it was between just the two of them now.

'You were going to tell me why you killed Charlie,' he said gently.

'I was out riding an' I met him. I often met him when I was out riding. He was always pretty friendly with me. This time he showed me the dust an' told me about the big claim he had found. I asked him if he would give me a share of his claim and he said what would a kid like me want with gold? He was just joking, I guess — I've realized that since — he never laughed at me like other people did. But I pulled my gun on him. People didn't know I carried a gun. I kept it inside my shirt an' practised with it when I was out riding.

'I told Charlie he could give me that bag of dust, anyway, he must have plenty more. He thought I was fooling — he tried to take the gun out of my hand, so I shot him. I was sorry afterwards, but I thought nobody would laugh at me if I went to another town and changed the dust into money. Nobody laughs at you when you have money. I hid the dust under the floorboards in my room. I figured I'd wait till the fuss had died down, then I'd leave Lagos.

'I liked Tom Brenner. He did not act like I was somebody to be laughed at. Mebbe that's because he's kind of a cripple, too. When they were gonna lynch Brenner 'cos they thought he'd killed Charlie, I had to do something about it . . . '

'You were very brave to face that mob, Caspar,' said Simmonds. Maybe if he could lull the younker's suspicions, make him drop his guard, maybe he'd have a chance to get the drop on him . . . But that gun never wavered, nor did the gaze of those eyes, seeming to bore its way through Simmonds' body.

Caspar went on, monotonously. 'I'm telling you this now so you can go out an' tell the posse that Brenner is innocent. I know you don't like Brenner, but if you don't promise to do what I say, I'll kill you.'

'I'll do as you say, Caspar.'

'I'll make sure of that. I'm gonna ride part of the way with you before I leave you. If you send the posse out after me, they won't catch me.'

Caspar smirked a little. Simmonds figured this was a good sign. The youth was not sorry for what he had done any more. He was beginning to preen himself, to fancy himself as a cool, clever desperado.

Caspar went on. His voice was no longer toneless. He was bragging loudly. 'I'm ready to go. The bag of gold-dust is outside on my horse . . . '

'That was taking a chance, wasn't it? Somebody might steal it.'

That threw a crimp in Caspar's style. His eyes took on a sudden puzzled look.

Then he burst out: 'You're just trying to be clever, that's all. Who's gonna be around in the middle o' the night?' But Simmonds could see he had him rattled. The deputy said, 'If you want me to ride with you I'll have to get my horse. He's out front. I'll have to get him round back somehow, huh?'

'Yes,' said Caspar. He nodded vigorously. 'Yes.' He slid from the desk and moved lopsidedly nearer to Simmonds.

'Turn around an' go out. Lead your horse up the alley. Remember I'm right behind you.'

Simmonds did as he was told. As he opened the office door, he hoped Louise Cantell was not on her way to meet him. But the street was still deserted.

'Keep your hands away from your sides,' said Caspar, and kicked the door to behind him. 'Just grab the horse an' lead him.'

Again Simmonds did as he was told, moved towards the alley. Caspar was not a practised desperado: he should have taken the deputy's gun in the first place and drawn his fangs. For a moment, Simmonds felt a pang of contemptuous pity. But he knew that pity had no place in this set-up now. This rabid little skunk behind him had gunned down a harmless old-timer like a dog, never giving him a chance, putting four bullets in him, a madman's act.

The alley was dark, but not long. Simmonds knew it was now or never, now in this black stretch of a few hundred yards before they moved into the pale moonlight once more. Now or maybe never anymore, never anything anymore.

Jay Simmonds jerked at his horse's bridle and the beast instinctively swerved and, even as Caspar triggered, Jay was diving beneath the horse's belly and the slugs whined away along the alley. The deputy rose to his knees and now his gun was in his hand. He fired twice beneath the horse's belly and Caspar cried out and Jay saw the foreshortened bulk there at the other side of the horse and fired again to make sure.

The echoes died away. He waited a few seconds, his free hand on the horse's flank, gentling him. Then he crawled forward.

Caspar was dead: there was no doubt about that. It had all been pretty easy after all. But Simmonds was not particularly proud of himself and he worked fast and mechanically now.

He dragged the body up the alley and through the back door of the jail. Then he locked up. He took charge of the bag of gold dust. He shut Caspar's horse in the stable then mounted his own horse and rode down Main Street.

Louise was waiting for him. She said, 'I heard shooting.'

Simmonds thought fast; said, 'That was me. I didn't have a gun an' had to borrow the spare one from the office drawer. It's a pretty ancient piece an' ain't been fired in a coon's age. I tried it out in the alley to muffle the sound. I hope I didn't wake any of the folks.'

The girl seemed satisfied. She set the pace. They were going through the pass when they heard the shots. They halted their horses, who badly needed a breather, anyway.

'It came from up there.' The girl pointed.

'Yeh, I thought that. Brenner must've

holed up. You stay here with the horses, Louise, an' I'll climb up an' investigate.'

'We'll ground-hitch the horses,' said the girl firmly. 'We'll both climb.'

Simmonds admired the girl's guts and wished momentarily that he was in Brenner's shoes. He hoped, for her sake, that the gimpy-legged fighting man was still alive. He led the way and pretty soon they came to the large ledge where the posse had left their horses. There had been no more firing, but now, as they stood trying to get their bearings, a single shot cracked from above.

'Come on,' said Louise urgently.

They came so suddenly upon Lemmy and Coney that they almost got themselves shot.

'What the hell . . . ?' began Lemmy Dricourt. Then he saw the girl and apologized for his language.

'Where's Josh?' asked Simmonds.

He was told that the sheriff and the rest of the bunch were making their way down the rocks like flies. It was a long and painful business, as they were being harried by the marksman down below all the time. They were still a long way from the valley floor.

15

'Yeh, I guess it's the posse, all right,' said Rory Jones. 'They've got one or two marksmen up top, I guess, while the rest are coming down to attack us. I'm sure that one we just saw in that patch of moonlight was Josh Penrose. I could've drilled him clean.'

Tom Brenner's white teeth flashed in the darkness. 'But you didn't.'

'Neither did you,' expostulated Rory. 'Heck, we certainly are a pair of mamby-pamby bandits. I ought to've at least shot Josh's hat off, the measly ol' goat.' He raised his rifle to his shoulder. 'Look, there goes another one.' He fired and the figure disappeared in a patch of shadow against the rock face.

A slug whined viciously from above and smacked into the corner of the cabin.

'They've certainly got us pinned

down here,' said Tom Brenner. 'That *hombre* up there is a shooting fool.'

'It's probably Coney,' said Rory. 'That fat freak's the best marksman in the territory.'

Brenner moved nearer to the corner. 'This is my fight, Rory,' he said. 'You've had enough of it. I'm going out there.'

'Don't be a fool,' Rory grabbed his arm and hauled on it. The old man was surprisingly strong. They strained in the darkness.

'Stay back, Rory,' panted Brenner. 'For God's sake, stay back. I don't want your blood on my head, too.'

'Let me go out,' grunted Rory. 'I'll explain things.'

'They'd shoot you down . . . Ugh!'

Rory had looped his long arm around the young man's throat and was pulling at him, bending him over backwards. Brenner squirmed like an eel. There was silence all around them now except for their panting breath. It was as if the men out there were waiting for the outcome of the struggle and the very hills were waiting, too. It was an elemental struggle, it fitted the mood of things, it was even getting a little savage now.

The old-timer had the strength of a bull. Brenner, a little weakened by earlier tussles and by his wounded head, felt for a moment almost impotent before him. This fact awakened the younger man's latent savagery and he got one arm free and struck out with a clenched fist. The blow, more by accident than design, caught Rory on the vulnerable angle of his jaw. The old man's grip relaxed and he went down.

A spasm of contrition went through Brenner, making him almost physically sick. He got down on one knee beside the old man. Rory grunted a little. But he was evidently unconscious.

Brenner rose and turned. He went round the corner. Walking not too fast, not too slow. Limping. His gun was still in his hand, hanging at the length of his arm. He let it fall. He began to swing his arms, his head erect. He had been a soldier once. His gimpy leg irritated him now because it prevented him from walking smartly. He wanted to go out smartly.

He was dramatising things, play-acting a little with an almost cynical detachment. That way he could keep his courage. Many men had called him brave, but he did not consider himself a particularly brave man. Things were stacked against him too strongly now. Things happened that way. His way of life had led him to this inevitability. It had been kill or be killed, but now he was all through with killing. Better to go out this way maybe, than behind blazing guns, taking a couple of young bucks with him, others of a long line of young bucks who had insisted on testing the 'master's' speed. He was little more than a buck himself, but he felt as old as the hills.

He was almost half-way across the clearing when he heard old Rory calling his name. He was glad to hear that voice, to know that the old man was not badly hurt, that he would leave one friend behind him here. But also, the voice had broken the spell and when it died there was silence again.

Out of the shadows in front of Brenner two people stepped and came slowly forward into the moonlight. For a moment, Brenner thought he was looking at some moonlit mirage. Then, afterwards, a strange feeling, half of anger, half-sorrow, came over him. What was Louise Cantell doing with Jay Simmonds? Then, behind them, he saw Josh Penrose, his empty hands hanging at his sides, just the way Simmonds' hands were hanging. Simmonds lengthened his stride and the girl hung back, almost shyly it seemed.

The two young men, both with bandaged heads, came face to face.

Simmonds held out his hand. 'I owe you an apology, Captain Bennett,' he said.

Tom took the hand, gripped it. He was still a little bemused. Simmonds told him quickly of the discovery of the folder, Caspar's confession and death. By this time, the sheriff and Louise had joined them and so had the other old-timer from the opposite direction.

'Rory, you old mossyback,' carolled Josh Penrose. The two oldsters shook hands enthusiastically.

'You all right, Rory?' asked Tom Bennett.

'A little smack on the jaw never hurt anybody. I'll hafta teach you to box properly.'

'Everything's all right, then,' said Tom Bennett softly. It hardly seemed possible.

The rest of the men were trickling down from the rocks. Bern Cantell put his arm around his daughter's waist.

'That was a foolish thing you did, *chiquita*,' he said softly. 'Coming out here like that.'

'But you understand, father?'

'Yes, I understand.'

'Why didn't you tell us who you were in the first place?' the sheriff asked Tom Bennett.

'I was fiddle-footing and I came to this territory to seek Charlie Bennett, who was my father's brother. I had not seen him for many years and had a hankering to do so again. I thought I might like to join him an' sink stakes in this territory for a while. I found him all right. You know how I found him. I figured that if I kept my identity secret — my name being Bennett, too — I'd have a better chance to find the killer. Of course, I did not expect the coincidence of the bank robbery an' all the rest of it.'

'And now I don't suppose that, after the way you've been treated, you feel inclined to sink stakes in this territory?'

'Well, I dunno . . . ' Tom Bennett was not looking at the sheriff anymore, but at Louise Cantell.

Bern Cantell said sonorously, 'Captain Bennett, I am sure that I am speaking for all citizens of Lagos when I offer abject apologies for the great injustice we have done you. The people of Lagos may be a little wild, but they are good people at heart. If you consent to stay among us, it will give us a chance to do everything in our power to wash away the wrong we have done . . . '

Louise Cantell stepped forward and held out her hand. Bennett took it. He had hardly heard a word that Bern had said, anyway. It was as if there was nobody else there now but the girl and himself.

'What my father is trying to say, Tom, is that we want you to stay with us.'

'I'll stay,' he said.

He did not have to say anything else.

THE END

Other titles in the
Linford Western Library:

A TOWN CALLED
TROUBLESOME

John Dyson

Matt Matthews had carved his ranch out of the wild Wyoming frontier. But he had his troubles. The big blow of '86 was catastrophic, with dead beeves littering the plains, and the oncoming winter presaged worse. On top of this, a gang of desperadoes had moved into the Snake River valley, killing, raping and rustling. All Matt can do is to take on the killers single-handed. But will he escape the hail of lead?

RODEO RENEGADE

Ty Kirwan

When English couple Rufus and Nancy Medford inherit a ranch in New Mexico, they find the majority of their neighbours are hostile to strangers. Befriended by only one rancher, and plagued by rustlers, the thought of returning to England is tempting, but needing to prove himself, Rufus is coached as a fighter by a circus sharp shooter, the mysterious Ghost of the Cimarron. But will this be enough to overcome the frightening odds against him?

GAMBLER'S BULLETS

Robert Lane

The conquering of the American west threw up men with all the virtues and vices. The men of vision, ready to work hard to build a better life, were in the majority. But there were also work-shy gamblers, robbers and killers. Amongst these ne'er-do-wells were Melvyn Revett, Trevor Younis and Wilf Murray. But two determined men — Curtis Tyson and Neville Gough — took to the trail, and not until their last bullets were spent would they give up the fight against the lawless trio.